Touchy Feely Sweet Thing

Kieran Frank

Winnipeg, Canada

Editors: Craig Gibb &: Alison Cybe

Published November 2023 by Deep Hearts YA, an imprint of Deep Desires Press and Story Perfect Inc.

Deep Hearts YA
PO Box 51053 Tyndall Park
Winnipeg, Manitoba R2X 3B0
Canada

Visit deepheartsya.com for more great reads.

Touchy Feely Sweet Thing

Chapter 1

The morning after Labor Day was my first day of senior year at Lac du Pac Public School. It was also the first school year I'd actually been left alone, even for wearing a plaid button-up that was out of fashion until it probably wasn't someday. No weird stares, no suspicious snickers, no annoying smirks on bullies' faces... Actually, where *were* the bullies this school year, anyway? Not that I was complaining. Maybe now that all the mean seniors had graduated and gone to college, the popular kids who remained just happened to be less mean.

That was a relief.

Also, no more Derry Dingleberry or Dingle Derry, thanks to Dad's last name, Derry. And since Mom's last name, Pico, wasn't immune to jokes, despite my preference for using it versus Dad's, I continued to go by just Jayden.

With my backpack over my shoulders, I walked through the small crowd in the administration wing to get to the high school wing. Kids of all grades passed me by. I still felt weird going back to school without my dyed-blond hair and blue eye contacts, since I normally went natural during the summer. Ollie Belasco had inspired me; he preferred me with dark hair and brown eyes. I wanted to believe I didn't have to anglicize my appearance that looked more Mediterranean than simply Latino.

I was about to walk past the counselor's office until something colorful by the open door captured my attention. I stopped and observed a sheet of paper taped to the wall. It had a rainbow header and looked like a signup sheet with a list of high school students' phone numbers.

My eyes widened, and my mouth dropped open. A proposal for an LGBTQ support group? *That* was new. I'd never in a million years expected something like that to exist in Lac du Pac Island. I could only picture a lot of parents outraged over the idea. Sadly, I wasn't surprised there were only three students listed on there—all girls—and I recognized their names. They were straight and cisgender as far as I knew, so they must've been allies. Besides me, Ollie, and Sasha Serrano, who else was here who'd actually *not* be straight and cisgender? Given that Sasha wasn't on there, she clearly didn't know about it because she would've definitely signed up.

Eh. What harm could it do to sign myself up too? It wasn't like I was in the closet, since practically the whole island knew I was gay, not that it wasn't stereotypically obvious by my mannerisms, gait, and voice. Hey, I wasn't ashamed of my mockable gender expression. Oddly enough, not many people knew I was asexual, but they probably didn't believe it was a thing.

I quickly grabbed a pen from my backpack. In the

"Available for personal contact?" section across the line, I circled "yes" because I had nothing better to do at home.

After my first three classes were done for the day, I entered the small cafeteria and waited in line at the food counter. Once I grabbed what I felt like eating, I carried my food tray in search of a table. There was a newly painted mascot logo centered on each wall, a step up from the plain walls. Dolphins, though. What an unusual choice when neither of those creatures even existed in Lake Huron. We northern Michiganders were way up by southern Canada, not bordering a single ocean. Still, I admired the nautically colored scheme that matched the rest of the building, and it complimented all of Lac du Pac Island as a touristy marine resort. As boring as my hometown was compared to all the action in the Lower Peninsula of mainland Michigan, especially being trapped with just a ferry or plane ride as the only escapes, it had its historical charm I'd never forget. If only the waters weren't still chilly in the summertime, though. I could use a nice dip of relaxation.

Sasha sat at our usual table with what looked like a catalog in front of her, and she played K-pop on her phone at a low volume.

Smiling, I took a seat across from her. The best thing about the new school year was that we had most of the same classes together, except she'd chosen pre-calc whereas I didn't have math anymore—thank *God*. Seniors didn't have to have a lunch period and could go home an hour early, but we'd figured we'd sit together in the cafeteria like old times, if just for that much-needed longer break between classes. For sharing one building, elementary school, middle school, and high school students each had their own lunch period in the same cafeteria, so it was always nice not having to eat with young children.

Sasha flipped her middle finger at someone while forming her signature bulldog facial expression. Combined with her towering height and big-boned figure, practically everyone was scared of her. Her big, brown eyes were narrowed in a threatening way at whoever it was, and she got back to her business. What had happened?

I turned and spied a couple of troublemakers as the remnants of the bullies' clique. Ugh, so maybe I hadn't been left alone *completely* this school year, since she'd most likely been defending *me* and not herself. Everyone knew never to mess with her, so of course, it'd been me as the target of mockery. It was why I felt safe whenever I was around her. With her excellent grades, it meant she was rarely absent from school, and she wore a mask if sick just to avoid missing school. I hated when she was absent, because it left me all alone to fend for myself, since teachers didn't always notice.

I glanced around the cafeteria, and something was strange. Where was Ollie? I even noticed Gracie Adkins and her judgmental church friends at their own table, which was at least where I'd have expected Ollie to sit if not with me and Sasha. I missed him already, and I looked forward to seeing him at school because it gave me an excuse to see him every day. We'd bonded over the recent days in a whole new way after losing touch for a few years. Now that he considered me his best friend, it made me feel more special, even though I couldn't quite do the same in return—Sasha would always win that spot. Ollie and I texted more than we called, so that his fanatically religious parents wouldn't eavesdrop, especially last night. We'd had many hours to ourselves, the longest we'd chatted without breaks. I in my room and he in his, all night just texting and sending stupid stuff with the occasional random picture and video clip of us thrown in.

I was relieved that Ollie was no longer the fanatical Christian he'd once been, having ditched those views a long time ago. Instead, he was a conservative Christian who kept his personal views to himself and who just happened to be gay like me. He knew better than to push me to go to church like he'd done in ninth grade before going our separate ways the next couple of years. After all, I'd never gone to church in my life, since neither of my parents had ever been religious.

But Christian or not, Ollie was *so* attractive and dreamy. I'd always thought he was cute in an adorable sort of way, but he was much more so than I'd ever imagined he'd be, given his former lankiness. He didn't fail to melt me in a way I'd only begun to feel over the summer. The nerdy posh look with trendy glasses was a good fit for him, much better than when he'd just been unfashionably nerdy like a typical dull churchgoer. His brown hair was still combed, but it suited him. The athletic build he'd developed over the years was nice to think about from time to time, and his very tall height was a plus.

We hadn't brought up the accidental erection I'd caused him to have when we'd briefly been alone at Sasha's house yesterday. We'd swum in her pool right after that, talked about it to confirm that our friendship wouldn't be affected, and texted each other all night later on. It was like the erection had never happened. I continued to wonder what it had meant because Ollie had always been respectful and only wanted to be friends, but for me to have evoked that kind of physical response out of him told me he thought about me as more than just a friend. That was the thing, though. Friends didn't get boners for each other, so he must've been hiding something that he wasn't comfortable admitting.

Like *I* was hiding the fact that Ollie could very well be my new squishy-crushy-something. What I felt for him wasn't exactly platonic. Well, not completely. Ugh, why was this so complicated?

Sasha's page turning captured my attention, especially the glossy and colorful pages. I grabbed a fry and glanced at the catalog of a college she was interested in. "What school is that?"

"It's in Texas." She tucked her dark curls behind her ears whenever they fell over her face when looking down. She was so focused that it made me realize how unimportant college had been to me over the years.

I noticed the name. "You're not going to *the* Texas University?"

"Oh, I am, but I love looking at these catalogs. I have, like, *fifty* of them at home. They just animate me. I don't know why." She smiled, her eyes glued to the high-quality pictures. Despite having outgrown her old colorful persona as a fictitious ginger named Bunny Bates, full of cheesy bunny videos with a dramatically bubbly voiceover, she still had plenty of geek left in her.

"Ooh, he's cute." I pointed at a college student posing near a large water fountain. He carried a stack of books while forming a presumably paid smile.

"Yeah, I can see that. Really sweet face to look at, I agree." It was so foreign to me how Sasha couldn't feel anything romantic for anyone, but *my* lack of sexual interest was probably the same confusion for most everyone else, what with being asexual and all. Ever since she'd come out to me as aromantic, I knew the meaning behind her strong aesthetic attraction to cute and sweet faces, especially famous guys she often shipped together in whatever fanfic she read nowadays. She also loved her share of SFW Boys' Love media, so there was that.

"Jaydles, I've noticed you haven't been talking about college at all. Are you even going next fall?"

I shrugged. "You already know I don't like school, and my grades aren't the best. I mean, they're okay, but I'd probably be stuck going to a community college if I do go."

"There's nothing wrong with that, though. It'll still open up many doors for you when it comes to jobs and careers. There're even career programs you can consider if you don't want an associate degree."

"Yeah, I know."

"But if you do plan to go, you should start making all the preparations you need now that we're seniors. Take the ACT or SAT like I did and start applying to different colleges."

"Yes, Mistress." I didn't want to stay on the topic

anymore because it was pointless, not to mention boring. "By the way, did you see the new signup sheet by the counselor's office? They're trying to gather enough support for an LGBTQ group."

Sasha's eyebrows flew up. "Really? How did I *not* know this?"

"It's a new thing. I just noticed it this morning."

"I'm totally signing up for that!"

"Yeah, you should. You just write your name, your phone number, email, and circle 'yes' or 'no' to be personally contacted."

"It's about time, honestly. This island is *so* conservative about that stuff, it's annoying."

I gasped as soon as an Emma Emmy song started playing on Sasha's phone. "Ooh, did you check out the tour dates for her *first* world tour?"

"Yeah, she'll be in Michigan in March."

I pouted. "I wish I could go but it's *all* the way in Detroit and we're *all* the way up here on our *nowhere* island."

Sasha sighed. "Aw, Jaydles, I feel your pain, I do, but to be fair, Lac du Pac Island *does* get a boatload of tourists every summer. I mean, it *is* a resort, so, yeah."

"Okay, Miss Pedantic. You knew what I meant." I lit up with excitement. "Anyway, Emma Emmy will always be my favorite singer in the world. She's just *so* awesome."

Sasha made an enthusiastic smile. "I agree, no one will *ever* be like her. Emmynions for life!"

"She has a ton of dance remixes too. I have them *all*, of course."

"I only have the popular one for 'On E.' Not really a

huge electronic dance music girl myself unless it's more on the K-pop side, but that one's a cool exception."

I grabbed another fry and glanced around the cafeteria. Kail Chase entered my mind, and I was relieved he was in college for his first year. I wouldn't have to see him again. Considering how he'd turned out to be, it was definitely a good thing—no, a *great* thing. Because we'd hooked up for three summers in a row, and it had meant so much to me, I'd never forget about him. It sucked that he'd had to hurt me the way he had. I'd been nothing but a piece of meat in his mind, and I'd reluctantly given it to him when I would've otherwise preferred a completely nonsexual relationship. It didn't matter that it'd been only minor stuff. Sex was still sex, and I didn't want any of it. I wanted love, instead. Then again, he'd never wanted anything serious to begin with, so it had all been a waste of time, much to my pain.

"Sash, I still think about Kail sometimes. He's in college now."

She still looked at the catalog but "telepathically" knew the very expression on my face. "Oh, Jaydles, I know it's been over a month since you stopped seeing him. You really should get over him for your own sake. I worry about you."

I sighed, making a slight pout.

"Please try? I imagine it's hard, since it's not something I'll ever be able to experience myself, but he was *really* toxic, and he tried to force himself on you. It's great you blocked him, though, which I'm sure helps."

Sasha was right about that. It helped to see Kail's true colors because only then was I finally able to be free from the hold he'd had on me. I was still a virgin back there, though, and it was something I was so relieved not to have given up to him, even though he'd been hungry for it for so long. The idea of being a virgin for life as a personal choice meant the world to me.

I wanted to forget about everything and move on, but at the same time, I wanted closure. Why was he the way he was when he'd never been that way before? What had changed? Or had he always been that way and had managed to fool me so easily?

I was a pathetic fool, after all.

"Besides," Sasha added, perking up. "You have Ollie now. And I know you guys are *just* friends, but I think you two would make the cutest and most awesome couple in the world. I totally ship you guys."

I tried not to blush at that idea but failed. While I'd never exactly admitted to anyone about my romantic curiosity or even the crush I had on Ollie, I wasn't surprised she could sense it in her own mystical sort of way. She was good at reading people, after all.

I took another glimpse of Gracie's table and frowned. Where *was* Ollie? It was the first day of senior year, so how could he have missed it? Unless he was at the library? Then again, I hadn't even seen him anywhere at school. There was a strong chance we didn't have any classes together, which would suck if that were the case.

"Sasha, has Ollie texted you?"

She shook her head. "I was actually going to ask you why he didn't show up today. I thought maybe you knew."

"No. We texted each other all night yesterday, but that was the last I heard from him."

She stopped focusing on her catalog and grinned. "*All* night?"

Ugh, I was blushing again.

"Jaydles, even though you've never told me how you felt, I'm not stupid. I know you like him. It's *so* obvious." Why was I not surprised she'd figured it out? This was Sasha here.

I sighed, feeling defeated. I usually told her everything, but my developing crush on Ollie was something I'd wanted to figure out on my own first. "I do like him. And I'm definitely ready to move on from Kail. I just don't know how he really feels about me."

"Honestly? I think he feels the same. I observe more than you know. I may be aro, but I'm not oblivious. I can recognize these things if they're overt." She dabbed her temple a few times in a duh expression.

"Okay, Miss Expert."

"Look, I just want you to be happy, and I think Ollie's a great choice for you."

"Yeah, well, if he didn't stop coming to school." I frowned.

"Maybe he's sick?" Sasha shrugged, then finally got back to the catalog.

I glanced at Gracie's table once more, and I suddenly had to find out what had happened, given that they attended the same church and talked to each other plenty of times. They used to be close when he'd been in the ninth grade and she in the sixth. Ugh, I didn't want to have to talk to *her*, especially since we'd never liked each other since day one. Now that she was a ninth grader, I'd see more of her until I graduated. I'd never forget her radical Christian views and strong stance against homosexuality. Just the fact that she was deeply involved in the Family Focus Forever Foundation because of her parents was nauseating enough. I knew not *every* Christian was like her, but she definitely made it easy to want nothing to do with Christianity. Still, I had to talk to her. I'd wait until after lunch to avoid making a scene.

I hoped Ollie was okay.

Chapter 2

After lunch, I walked through the high school wing and spied Gracie at her locker with her two ninth grade friends, the same two girls who'd sat with her at Lac du Pac Island State Park a few weeks ago. Wasn't the Black girl named Melanie Mitchell? She was memorable not just for being Black—given the island's demographics—but also because of her beauty product commercial face with a super-white smile. I forgot the other one's name, though—a cockie-cutter blonde girl who was kind of forgettable.

The three of them always wore dull tops and ankle-length skirts, and I imagined it was a sin for them to cut their ridiculously long hair that might as well be in bonnets. Okay, so maybe I was a *tad* judgmental myself, but I was convinced they judged me way more than I judged them. Even their eyes darted my way as I trudged toward them, like I was a moral threat to them.

Whatever.

I inhaled and tightened my expression into an uncomfortably fake smile, and I drew a breath. "Hey...I was just wondering if you knew where Ollie's been. I haven't seen him at school today, not even at lunch."

Gracie arched an eyebrow as if questioning why I'd dare to ask, her pigtailed self always acting like the star of the group. "Why do you want to know that?" Hostile much? Then again, what else was new? Her friends looked like they were the sheep trying to mimic her reactions. Whether or not they agreed with her was a mystery.

"Um...because he's my friend?" Patience, Jayden, patience. Why was it hard to hide my defensiveness?

It took a moment for her to reply. "He was in the library for lunch period."

My eyebrows flew up, and my heart cracked a little because I suddenly felt like he'd been hiding from me. Why wouldn't he have told me that? Why had he even been *there*, anyway? Had he not wanted me to know where he'd been? It wasn't like him at all to avoid me, especially since we'd gotten along so well last night. Avoiding me wouldn't have made sense. Something wasn't right.

"Oh..." I managed. "But...he didn't go to any of his classes?"

"Of course, but he's not allowed to sit in the cafeteria for lunch until further notice. It's his parents' orders, not mine."

The former pretty much confirmed we didn't have any classes together, which meant he was in the other group, since every grade in our school was divided into two groups with as few students as there were here compared to most schools in the U.S. The latter, though? What exactly had happened? Was he grounded? I tried my best to mask my disappointment.

Gracie sighed. "I didn't want to say anything to you about that since it's really none of your business, but you asked. And since I'm a Christian, I'm not supposed to lie. Of course, you wouldn't *know* a thing about being a Christian, so I don't expect you to understand our values."

Her friends gave me the same icy stare.

I refrained from rolling my eyes. She could drown in her own iciness for all I cared—they *all* could.

"And please don't bother him anymore," Gracie added. "In fact, it's better if you pretend he doesn't exist because I already had to explain to his parents that it wasn't his fault what you did to him."

I wrinkled my forehead in confusion, and I didn't like the sound of that accusation. "What do you mean? What exactly did I do?"

"You're a bad influence, Jayden. I told his parents what I saw at the park."

Gracie's friends nodded like the witnesses they apparently were, still mute.

Ugh, what was she *talking* about! "Gracie, we were just hanging out that day. What did we do wrong? Like, seriously, I'm confused."

"*He* didn't do anything wrong. *You* did. You came on to him with your hand on his shoulder in an inappropriate way. You were trying to make him be like *you*."

...What? Oh, God. I'd placed my hand on Ollie's shoulder in a supportive way with no hidden intentions. Gracie had seen that, and she'd actually mistaken it as inappropriate? She had a lot of nerve to twist that around! "Ugh, you *really* misread that because we're *just* friends."

"I don't believe you. I'm not stupid. I see the way you check him out with those hungry eyes." Gracie formed a grimace.

"That is *not* fair. Why would you assume stuff like that?" She wasn't entirely wrong, since I *did* check Ollie out, just never in the way she insisted.

"I'm sorry, but boys like you can't be trusted."

Her friends shook her heads, agreeing with her in silence.

Boys like me. I panted silently, trying my hardest to control my anger. I stared at her and wondered why she was doing this to me. "Why do you hate me so much, Gracie? What did I ever do to you?"

"Hate is a strong word, and God wouldn't want me to hate anyone. I hate the *sin*, not the sinner."

"Oh, please, whatever. Like *you* don't sin. Oh, wait. Of course not. You're God's favorite little angel, and your favorite hobby is pointing fingers at others for being *sinners*."

"Please don't put words in my mouth."

I let out a sarcastic chuckle. "Funny you should say that. Maybe *you* should do the same instead of making crude assumptions. For your information, I'm asexual, so it's not even possible for me to be the kind of person you think I am toward Ollie."

Gracie lowered her eyebrows. "What does that even mean, or did you just make that up because you're a woke liberal?"

"A woke liberal? Seriously? And, no, I didn't make it up. I'm not sexually attracted to anyone. I can have romantic feelings for people, but that's the extent of anything nonplatonic." Wow, was I seriously educating her on asexuality? I hoped she'd get it.

"Well, I don't believe in that woke nonsense. And how do I know you're not just saying that to cover up the truth?"

"I don't *want* Ollie like that, Gracie. I *swear* I didn't touch him like that. He was upset about something, and I was just trying to cheer him up with a supportive gesture. That's the truth! I can't believe you'd make something like that up to hurt me."

"I'm not trying to hurt you. I know what I saw."

"No. You *don't* know." Oh. My. God. I wanted to knock some sense into her, or at least let *God* do it if he even existed. At the same time, the frustration made my eyes water because it was such a dangerous lie. I could get in trouble for sexual harassment when it hadn't even been the case.

I sighed. "You know what? Let's settle this right now. Ollie's probably still at the library, so I'll confront him about it. He'd never hurt me by making stuff up because he's an actual friend and we care about each other. He'll tell you the truth, you'll see."

"Th-that's not necessary," Gracie quickly said.

Oh? Was she nervous all of a sudden? She'd wasted no time saying *that*. I questioned whether she really had gotten the gesture confused, or if she'd made it up to get me in trouble.

She pursed her lips with reddened cheeks, and I wasn't

sure if she was angry or embarrassed—or both. "Maybe…I might have misread the gesture."

So, she'd made it up all along. There was no way her sudden change was a misunderstanding, especially after I'd insisted that we talk to Ollie.

I shook my head. "You could've gotten me in trouble with that. But then again, maybe that was the point." I gave her one last stare, an icy one just like hers, and I walked away. I'd already had little respect for her, and I suddenly had none. The fact that she'd come between me and Ollie was unforgivable. He'd never ignore me for no reason, so she'd sabotaged my friendship with him with a single lie.

Would I ever hear from Ollie again?

Chapter 3

Thursday morning marked three days since I'd last heard from Ollie. No texts, no calls, and I hadn't seen him at school, even though he apparently attended. What was going on? He'd never, ever ignore me, and nothing had happened between us to stop talking, especially since we'd gotten over his awkward erection. Had he really been grounded? I hated Gracie so much for what she'd done. She was supposed to be a Christian. Why would she do such a thing?

With my backpack over my shoulders, I walked through the small hallway crowd in the high school wing, still relieved that the majority of the students left me alone for the most part. I reached my locker and opened it, a deep frown spanning my face. I hadn't been this depressed since Kail had hurt me, and for some reason, I felt more so over possibly losing Ollie because he'd actually meant something real to me. He was a true friend, unlike Kail. I also couldn't stop thinking about Ollie. My feelings for him wouldn't go away.

I grabbed my textbook, shut my locker, and walked to

my first class. After my third of six classes was done, it was lunch period. Sasha had tried to cheer me up with a few anime videos, and it had only worked for so long before she'd given up and had had a talk with me about it. She hadn't heard from Ollie either, so she could at least relate.

After school, I was back at my locker, getting ready to go home. When I closed it and put my backpack on, there he was already approaching me with a serious expression.

My heart stopped for a moment, and the sight of him sucked all the air out of me. "Ollie!" I called in a breathy tone.

He always made me feel short, even though I was of average height, and I loved it. He looked around his shoulders, even though there was hardly anyone around right now, what with everyone rushing to get home. "Jayden, hi."

"I haven't heard from you, and I got worried."

"I know and I'm sorry. I wasn't ignoring you. I promise that's the truth."

I sighed in relief, even though I'd already had an idea that that hadn't been the case. "What's going on? I miss you."

"Aw, Jayden, I miss you too." He kept looking around as if alert, then lowered his voice. "But we can't be friends anymore." A frown played on his lips, and it sank my heart to the bottom to hear him say that and seeing it hurt him too.

My face pretty much mimicked his because I felt just as sad as he did. "But...why, Ollie? What happened?" I tried to be discreet with my voice as well.

"Gracie told my parents she saw you trying to make a pass at me at the park, and they freaked out and demanded that I stop talking to you. I can't be near you anymore. They took my phone away. I can't use the internet without being monitored."

Wow, so he'd been grounded, after all. What a terrible person Gracie was. Ugh, why would she do that!

"I can't even sneak out of the house anymore because she told them to be careful in case you influence me to do that, even though I only did it once when you and I hung out at the park, and no one but Sasha knows about that. You're apparently a bad influence. Can you believe it?"

God, how I hated Gracie so much. What benefit of hers was it to have destroyed my friendship with Ollie? It just made her into a bully, and I wished I could get back at her for it.

"You and I were supposed to be in the same group, actually, but my parents called the school and insisted that they switch me to the other group."

I scoffed, and of course, Gracie was most likely relishing it. "So, we could've had the same classes?"

"We could've, yes. I think I know why she did all this."

"Why?" I couldn't think of a single justification other than being a mean brat who'd been bored and had wanted to have fun because she could.

"I think she has feelings for me." Ollie's sad face tugged at my heartstrings.

"Oh…" Of course. Why hadn't I considered that before? It suddenly made sense. She'd probably suspected his sexuality and wanted to "save" him from *sin*, just so that she could have him all to herself. Then again, she wasn't alone in feeling something for him. I felt it too. We both did, and she'd won. She'd taken him away from me.

"Yes. At first, when I suspected a while ago, before you and I grew closer, I didn't think it was a real biggie. I ignored it because I figured she would get over it since she's younger. I was wrong. Now, it changes everything. I wouldn't be surprised if my parents start pressuring me to ask her out on a date since they've hinted at it before, which means they probably know about her feelings for me."

"But…she's in the ninth grade, isn't she? And you're in the twelfth. Your parents don't have a problem with that?"

"They don't, no. They don't see anything wrong with it at all."

I grimaced. "But she's fourteen! And you'll be eighteen in November!" Wow, it was a little creepy of Ollie's parents to accept. It was sad that they accepted *that* kind of relationship than a same-age gay one, just because it was straight.

"I know, but it doesn't bother them."

My depression worsened the more I heard about all that. I didn't really care if Gracie had feelings for him, since Ollie didn't feel the same way. It was more that her feelings happened to be the cause of her trying to keep us apart. "Did your parents read our texts?"

Ollie shook his head. "They didn't, no. I always delete our chats just to be safe."

"Thank God, at least. That's a relief."

"It is, yes. But they did see one video clip of you because

I thought I deleted all the pictures and videos you sent me. It made things worse, actually."

My heart raced. "Oh, no…which video?"

He swallowed. "It was one of you blowing a kiss at me."

I wanted to smack myself all of a sudden. That particular clip had just been me being silly, and Ollie had known it hadn't been serious, even though I'd subconsciously meant to do it because of my crush on him. He'd shocked me with a wink emoji as a response, along with a heart reaction to the clip, causing me to wonder how he'd really felt about it. His parents wouldn't have understood a thing about it, though. They'd always see it as me flirting with him like some dangerous seduction, and given all that Gracie had told them, the clip had served as fodder for their suspicions.

Because of course!

I heard loud footsteps as if stomping, coming from around the left corner straight ahead, and it sounded a little dramatic. "Ollie!" Wait, was that Gracie?

"Oh, great," Ollie muttered with a frown.

"I'm ready to go home, and I'm coming nearby!" Oh, my god, it was!

I looked at the corner and wondered if she'd been eavesdropping. Was she hiding? It was like she stomped a few times, stopped, stomped again, and then stopped, rinse and repeat. Why did she have to be so stupid about it? Why not just come over to us and say what she had to say?

"Jayden, I have to go," Ollie quickly said under his breath. The pained look on his face told me how much he missed me already. He really liked me just like I liked him, and it was over between us. A beautiful friendship, gone, just like that. He leaned toward my ear and whispered, "Please don't give up on us, okay?" His breath tickled my ear with warmth, and my heart melted from his words. "I'll be eighteen in November, so I can legally be on my own by then. My birthday is not far away at all, okay?"

"I know. I just…don't want you to go," I said in misery.

"I know, I know, but I have to. Always remember this. I've never stopped fighting for you, and I never will. We'll always be together, no matter what happens." Ollie finally walked away.

My heart cracked some more. Watching him leave was harder than I'd imagined because it meant things between us had changed forever, or for as long as we were on the island. College was our only hope at this rate, if I even wanted to go. He disappeared around the corner, and I heard their footsteps fading away. Ugh, Gracie had been hiding over there all along like a passive-aggressive coward, which explained the exaggerated stomping as a way to interrupt me and Ollie indirectly. She'd probably peeked at us at one point and hadn't wanted to see us be affectionate, not that we'd ever dare to be around here.

I leaned against the lockers nearby and lowered my gaze to the floor, my eyes starting to water. I had no choice but to move on from him, because while it didn't exactly mean a permanent goodbye, it did mean I wouldn't get to hang out with him until he left for college next fall. By now, there was no telling if we'd still be friends. I wanted to believe we'd be because of our strong bond, but anything could happen until then.

I finally walked away from the lockers and down the hallway where Ollie and Gracie had left from. When I exited the school building, I felt some fresh air from what had been a stifling moment of drama. The weather was a bit cool today, but it was tolerable. Instead of heading home, I turned left toward downtown, which was just a few hundred yards away. The gravel road turned into Main Street, which was brick throughout the entire downtown of historical shops, restaurants, and bars.

There were still many diverse tourists around and plenty of horse-drawn carriages galloping by. May to October were Lac du Pac Island's busiest months of the year, especially July and August. Sometimes, the heavy tourism was okay because it brought in a lot of revenue for the island. Most other times, it was annoying because I often wanted to take a stroll through downtown without having to deal with a large crowd.

The driver of a horse-drawn carriage whistled and waved at me as a common greeting to walkers, guiding the horses past me while tourists rode in the covered back.

I politely returned a princess wave with a weak smile. I hadn't ridden on one in quite a while since I preferred to walk. Since the horses were shipped back to the farms in mainland Michigan during the winter, walking and snowmobiling were the common forms of transportation. I still walked to school in the winter, though, bundled up and all. (The lake effect sucked.)

I strolled past the café where Ollie had come out to me with his sexuality a month ago, and I smiled a little at the memory. He'd been so nervous and distraught about it, and

I'd been there for him as the friend he'd needed. I missed him so much already, and thinking about losing him hurt more than I'd been prepared for. I missed our chats, I missed seeing him, and I missed hugging him. Granted, we hadn't hugged a whole lot, but the couple of times we had, it'd been so nice and warm, and he smelled so clean like soap. He didn't need any cologne, but when he wore some, it was more like a hint of it.

I decided to go to one of the candy shops to get a small block of the island's famous fudge, and I waited in line. The Asian boy ahead of me looked very familiar while he held hands with a white girl I'd seen many times. Within seconds, I remembered him. He was Jasper Chen from the DORK bond back in my freshman year, still dressed in all black and probably as quiet as he'd always seemed to be. He had to be a sophomore. He'd grown taller since then too. I hadn't seen him in a long time, but I hadn't paid too much attention to many people over the years. Being bullied on a regular basis kind of did that.

After Jasper paid for his order and grabbed a large bag of assorted candy, he turned around and walked right past me, still holding hands with who was presumably his girlfriend. Either I was *that* invisible or he hadn't recognized me without my dyed-blond hair and blue eye contacts. Sometimes, I wondered if I should go back to my old look, but Ollie's compliment about my natural look lingered in my head and made me smile like a dork. We were just friends, but that compliment really made me feel warm and special.

After placing my order, paying the clerk, and walking

away from the counter, I continued out of the shop and ate my fudge on the way back home. Ollie couldn't stop barging into my thoughts and making me sad, and I knew I had to do something as a distraction. I had homework to do later today, but it was too boring to look forward to. I wished I had a hobby like interesting people did, if just to have something to keep me busy.

The depression kicked into high gear, drooping my lips. Sometimes, I wondered why I even bothered with anything in life. Being born in the wrong town sucked because of how I was in a society I couldn't relate to. It had caused me enough trouble and had made it hard for me to make friends. I was lucky to have made a best friend in Sasha, but now that we were back in school, she'd been busy during the week. I didn't want to bother her when I knew she had homework and studying to do, just like *I* should've been doing. She'd probably agree to do it together, since we shared most of the same classes, and while we'd be spending time together, she'd also be intensely focused on it with no room for chit-chat or a little goofing off.

Boring!

Many minutes later, I got home and entered my room. I dropped my backpack on the floor and crashed on the bed, feeling totally unmotivated. Ugh, I didn't want to do any homework. Why did *all* my classes have to assign something today? It wasn't like that every day, but today had to be one of *those* days.

I looked at the pastel color scheme that surrounded me, and I still thought about giving my room a redesign. I wondered how expensive it'd be. Oh, well. Someday.

As I was about to start on the easiest of the assignments, my phone chimed with a text notification. I grabbed it and checked the screen.

Hi...I got your number from the LGBTQ signup sheet. I hate our town. I don't want to be a lesbian anymore. :(

I lowered my eyebrows. Another gay person in Lac du Pac Island? Who could it be? I'd seen just about all the girls at school of all grades, and while I didn't know every single one of them on a personal level, I'd most likely recognize her if the secret lesbian had revealed herself to me.

I knew the feeling all too well, though. Well, okay, maybe not wanting to change my sexuality, but definitely the struggle. I typed back a short reply expressing sympathy and that if she needed someone to talk to, she could contact me anytime. I got back to starting my first homework, and I hadn't heard back from her by the time I finished it.

I hoped I heard from her again.

Chapter 4

The next day, I got home from school and changed clothes to go to Sasha's house. Thank God it was Friday. I was caught up on my homework, so I didn't have to worry about it over the weekend. It was strange no longer hearing from Ollie. We hadn't chatted for years but had then grown closer this past summer. It'd been like a tease because our bond had formed, only for it to be taken away for homophobic reasons.

I also hadn't heard back from the secret lesbian. I really wished she could text me again so that I could show her some support in whatever way I could. I wanted her to realize she wasn't alone and that she couldn't change who she was. I hoped she was okay.

I walked out of my room. Mom was on the long couch against the other side of my bedroom wall, fiddling with a pack of cigarettes. She was dressed up for the bar. She must've retouched her dyed-blond hair earlier today since her dark roots had recently started growing, and like I used to, she sometimes wore blue contacts to mask her brown eyes. She was still pretty for her age, even though she'd partied way too hard with alcohol and drugs just about every weekend, sometimes on weeknights.

As a result, I hadn't felt like she was a mom in years, and after Dad had left us three years ago, I didn't think I'd ever see the mother in her again. I missed seeing that side of her. Was she over Dad? She'd dated and hooked up with lots of men, and since she didn't seem sad about it anymore, it was hard to tell.

Not that I wanted Dad back in our lives. He'd walked out on us, after all, so he could stay gone. At least, she still had her job as a clerk at the local general store, albeit downgraded from her former manager position at a bank. Partying hard and getting fired over it did that, and I only hoped it wouldn't cost her the current job she held. How else would she support us?

Mom lit up a cigarette and blew some smoke. "I have to hurry and get to the ferry before the last ride leaves," she said in her smoker's voice that didn't match her attractive appearance. "I'll be gone all weekend. I brought some groceries, so you should be good until then."

I shrugged. "Sure, okay, yeah. Have fun." She most likely was going to party in mainland Michigan, but I wasn't sure what city.

"Bye." She apathetically walked out of the house and rushed down the gravel road. It was one of the few times I saw her sober, but of course, that wouldn't last by nighttime.

I stepped out and locked the door, starting on my way to Sasha's house. The warm sunrays kissed my skin, and it sucked that the weather wouldn't last much longer in September.

It was always worth leaving the house, though. My road was among the downscale parts of the island, not that it was completely rundown. Small cottages and shotgun shacks made up the homes here, none of them with basements like the large Victorian houses on Sasha's upscale road had. All the houses in her neighborhood had spacious yards and manicured gardens, and the beautiful environment there exuded a comfortable atmosphere, hence one of the major reasons I liked visiting the area. The large lake houses on the main road, however, were the wealthiest of the island, and I couldn't financially afford to even dream about living there.

I remembered when Sasha and I had once attempted to walk around the main road that circled the island, but eight miles was just too far of a walk under the hot sun, so we'd only managed about halfway, all sweaty and gross. Still, it'd been nice seeing the view of Lake Huron. Sometimes, we'd go to the rocky edge of the lake and admire the view from a closer distance. If only Lac du Pac Island had a proper beach instead of rocks all around, and the chilly water during the summer didn't help, what with the island being so far north near Canada.

I reached Sasha's house and ambled through the right side. I opened the gate and stepped inside the backyard where a sweaty Sasha was beating up a punching bag with boxing gloves and her strong legs. She hadn't practiced kickboxing in a long time. What made her feel like trying it out again? I knew she wasn't interested in it as a career, but it was still fun to watch her be so devoted to practicing it. It made me realize how much I needed a hobby. She didn't just kickbox, but she baked, watched tons of anime, listened to a lot of bubbly music, read many fanfics online, played numerous video games, and she spent enough quality time with her family on top of all that. In other words, she always found something to do with her time when she wasn't busy with school stuff.

She stopped and glanced at me with a smile. "Hey, Jayden." She wiped some sweat off her forehead with her forearm.

"You're still really good at that."

"Thanks. I'm not serious about it, at least not actually doing anything with it in my life. I like to keep learning how to protect myself because you never know who you can meet out there."

That brought memories of Kail. The last time I'd seen him was a bit scary because he'd tried to get me to have sex with him in his room with the lights off. His hormones knew no boundaries, and he'd even warned me that he might've not been able to control himself once he started. While he had eventually stopped when I'd told him enough times, it served as a warning of what kinds of guys I could easily meet if I wasn't careful.

Staring at the punching bag, I frowned at the reality of my situation. It sucked being physically weak.

Sasha smiled more strongly. "Want to try?"

I let out a halfhearted laugh. "Like I could *ever* be as good as you."

"Not *now*, but maybe one day. Besides, it's not about being good. It's about protecting yourself." She formed a frown. "I worry about you, Jaydles."

The more I stared at the punching bag, the more it made me wonder if I could ever grow some kind of strength. It definitely didn't hurt to try, and it wasn't like I had anything better to do. "I guess I can give it a shot."

"Yay, finally!" Sasha was giddier than she needed to be, but it was nice that *someone* was at least happy. "Since my gloves are too big for you, we can start with kicks."

"Sure, okay, yeah." I knew I'd suck. I watched her demonstrate a sidekick, and she made it look easier than it probably was. I tried to mimic her, but my body moved out of balance, not at all as stiff as hers. I was able to kick the punching bag, but because it was so hard and heavy, it might as well have kicked *me*.

"It just takes a lot of practice. Believe me, I wasn't born with the skill. I just happened to learn at a young age. Since my dad never had sons, he was overjoyed when I took an interest in this kind of stuff. My two sisters are *way* too feminine and don't like to do any of this. That *said*, they did learn to fight for self-protection. My dad taught the three of us. It was pretty much a requirement, so we had no choice."

Even Sasha's older sisters knew how to fight more than I did with as feminine as they were. It made me feel more embarrassed, like my life was just that much sadder all of a sudden. I really was a pathetic weakling.

"Come on, try again." Sasha was so persistent. She'd waited for this moment for so long, after all.

I did and almost lost my balance, wincing from what felt like kicking a brick wall. Several more tries, I failed again. I gave it my all the last few times and failed yet again.

Ugh, I was ready to give up. I stopped and tried to catch my breath, my forehead starting to sweat.

Sasha gave me a shrug. "It could take weeks, months, years, depending on the person. You won't improve overnight, but at least you tried more times than I thought you would, which is a start."

"I'm not cut out for this."

"Eh. Not everyone is, but that's why you have to keep at it. Ever since you told me about your last hangout with Kail, I just started worrying because of how lucky you were that he eventually stopped. Not every guy is like that."

"I know." Maybe one day I'd get back at it again, but for now, I needed to relax and think about something else. "So, Geoff is coming next week?" Not that I cared about the new foreign exchange student from Germany, but it was a change of topic, nonetheless.

Sasha beamed. "Yep! We're picking him up on Sunday, and he'll be starting school with us the next day. I'm so animated!"

It was weird how excited she was for a total stranger to stay with her and her family for four months. I couldn't relate to that at all. Not only would I need my space, since there wasn't any room at home for anyone else, but I'd have to learn to trust someone I didn't know living in my house, even if temporarily.

I tried to be happy for her, and I wanted to be. It was just hard to get over the fact that I wouldn't be able to sleep in the guestroom anymore, and sharing a bed with Geoff was totally out of the question, not that he'd even want to. With a bathroom next door and a little bar next to the kitchenette against the back wall, it was like living in my own apartment whenever I stayed the night. Maybe everything would turn out okay. Maybe I'd get over it and welcome him the same way Sasha would.

Hopefully, anyway.

Chapter 5

On Monday morning, I returned to school a second time, after being sent home for wearing a shirt that read, *Boy(senberry) Juice = Protein*. I'd thought I'd try to risk it because it wasn't an obvious pun to everyone, but I should've known that particular shirt left a bitter taste for the faculty.

Thoughts of Kail returned for the umpteenth time, and rather than the usual bliss, a spritz of melancholy and resentment took place. A boy's first love was a huge deal, and in my case, it was a huge deal *and* a total disaster. Ugh, he was supposed to be dead to me after what he'd done. Why couldn't I get over him for good?

I shoved away the thoughts of him and smiled as soon as I saw Sasha fumbling through her locker. She'd been busy outside of lunch period, and while we shared most of the same classes, she took school *way* too seriously to chill out with me in class once in a while.

An unfamiliar guy stood beside her, and he looked a lot like Ollie in an eerie way. Well, not so much in the face except for having warm, brown eyes, and definitely not as athletically built, but more so with the same brown hair that was also combed, the same kind of nerdy posh outfit, and the same kind of trendy glasses. Was that Geoff? I wasn't sure if I should give Sasha some space, but I knew better than not to be open-minded. After all, my tiny circle of friends couldn't hurt to include a new third. Or fourth? Who knew when Ollie would join us again?

"Hey, guys." I gave them a princess wave, ready to meet the new guy.

Sasha waved back, a bit too giddily. "Hey, Jaydles!" Yep, it *had* to be Geoff. Why else would she be giddy around him?

He formed an overjoyed expression, showing the kind of teeth that proved he regularly took care of himself. Wow, he really did have many of Ollie's features, and he was only a little shorter than Ollie, but not by much. They didn't look related, of course, but still. From what I could tell by looking at his arms and his body shape through his clothes, he was lean but with more tone than my twig body could ever dream of having.

He gave me a little wave in return. He was *really* happy to meet me. He seemed friendly, at least, and that could never be a bad thing.

"Jayden, this is Geoff…" Sasha paused and glanced at him. "…*Böchmann*, right?" She pronounced it as "BEUGH-mon" with a guttural sound, but who knew if it was correct?

"Yah, but it's okay," Geoff said in a strong German accent. "It's not to fear. You're not terrible when you talk German. No problems." He had a soothing voice, not quite as deep as Ollie's, but nice, nonetheless. He looked at me and extended a hand for a shake. The polite manners were unlike most students, especially since he was fifteen and not much older to justify the formal gesture. Even his smile seemed genuine. Then again, maybe he was just doing it here in the U.S. because he felt pressured to. I wasn't sure if they greeted each other that way in Germany.

Still, I shook his hand, feeling slightly awkward with the formality.

Sasha beamed. "Geoff's the foreign exchange student from Germany I told you about, and like I mentioned, he's staying at my house for a semester. Well, until New Year's Eve, so *almost* a semester since the next one starts in mid-January."

"Oh, right." I'd already known that, but I figured Sasha was just making conversation. I hoped he'd be fine with my sexuality since I knew most people's gaydar alerted them whenever they were around me. Oh, wait, wasn't he liberal from Berlin? Either way, while I couldn't care less about such petty things in general, I didn't need a bigot hanging out with *my* best friend. Thankfully, that wouldn't be the case with him. I also remembered he wasn't religious, which helped, since Sasha and I weren't.

"And don't worry, he knows." Sasha winked at me as if telepathic.

"Yah, I have much gay friends in Germany since before a few years, and I really much like them because they're so very nice persons. I'm not bothered never by those things like the bigots are always." His accent was thankfully clear the more he spoke, just that the way he phrased things was odd. He definitely needed to work on his grammar, though, but I didn't want to be rude and point it out. He probably tried his hardest, after all, though I'd heard plenty of Germans online who spoke better English. Maybe it was more of a Geoff thing too.

I sighed in dramatic relief just because. "Love your attitude!" I chuckled along with Sasha and Geoff, but it came out a bit more contrived than I'd intended. Still, it really was a relief to know he was a cool person, so far. Maybe we could be friends, after all?

Geoff flashed an enthusiastic smile as his response. Okay, the more I noticed him, the more I had to admit that, had it not been for how I felt about Ollie and for Geoff being straight, I could easily have a crush on Geoff. He was *so* attractive. If Ollie was my type, so was Geoff. Yep, they did resemble each other *that* much. Maybe I actually had a type now.

The look on Sasha's face was priceless. "He's teaching me some German too. It's super hard, but I'm trying my best."

"It's okay, Sasha," Geoff said. "I understand still when you talk German."

"Yay! Also, we've been spending *so* much time together, Jaydles. We're practically inseparable already." She formed a toothy grin.

I paused, suddenly feeling a little pinch in my heart. That explained why she'd seemed extra busy yesterday, too busy to have me over. I tried my hardest to be happy for her because having a foreign exchange student was a dream come true for her. She'd wanted one for a while, especially a live-in brother, and she finally got it. I just wished it didn't make me feel like this.

Different.

"He's *so* intelligent and *nice*," she added. "And just *awesome*. I can't wait to bake cookies and brownies with him tonight." She glanced at Geoff. "With lots of frosting, right?"

"Yah, of course. Frostings are yummy."

"*Noice.*" Noice? Ugh, really, Sasha? And they were baking cookies and brownies without me? Given that she was so good at baking, Geoff would definitely fall in love with her sweet treats like I had. All of a sudden, I didn't dare to ask if I could join them because I felt uninvited. She always invited me over for stuff like that. What had changed?

I flashed a set of clenched teeth, forming the fakest smile that made a celeb's face seem genuine. The inside showed otherwise, though. What else could I say?

"I'm so animated! It'll be like a slumber party except we can't really stay up late because it's on a school night."

A slumber party too?

"The only thing is that he's now staying in the guestroom." Sasha twisted her lips in an apologetic expression. "So, if you ever stay the night again, you'll have to sleep on the sofa."

If I ever stayed the night again? Whatever happened to *when* I stayed the night again? I didn't like the sound of that at all, and it was becoming more challenging to hide how I felt. I also hated that Geoff had officially taken over the guestroom until New Year's Eve, even though I'd already known he would. It sucked!

That was *my* room!

"Oh, okay." I managed, my voice a bit weak. Sasha might have officially found a replacement that blindsided me like no other blindside in life, according to the giddiness that plagued her face and all the fun plans and slumber parties abound. What was wrong with just the two musketeers if Ollie couldn't be with us anymore? Geoff's presence suddenly proved three was a crowd.

Nope. He and I couldn't be friends.

Chapter 6

O n Sunday evening, after a whole week of barely talking to Sasha, I was finally at her house eating in the dining room with her, her parents, and Geoff. Her two older sisters were back in college, and while they technically lived at home, they had to stay in the dorms while in school because of the distance.

It felt like an eternity since I'd last come over. Ugh, but I wished I could smile wider every time she praised Geoff in front of the whole family. It reminded me of when she'd done that to *me* back in freshman year when we'd first met and had become friends right away. Just because he was from another country didn't make him special all of a sudden. Sure, he was probably the brother Sasha had never had, but it was still unnecessary.

Besides, what about *me*? *I* could be her (sisterly) brother. It was bad enough that I still hadn't heard from Ollie, not that I expected to. (Well, technically, I hadn't lost either of them, but still.)

I was almost finished with my meal, and it was *so* tasty. Sasha's mother had prepared chicken enchiladas, chiles rellenos, fried rice with tomato chunks, and refried beans, with flan to come for dessert. It was always a treat to get to eat authentic Mexican food, as filling as it was. Sasha had already taken a picture of her plate of food with her phone to upload it online with all the other ones she'd taken. It was also amazing how welcoming her family had always been, which wasn't a surprise that Geoff was instantly a part of the family, something that had only been reserved for me.

Everyone enjoyed themselves with such a naturally healthy ambience that filled the spacious room, but I wasn't feeling it. In just a couple of hours, Mom would be waiting for me to come home with her pseudo emotions that seemed more like disguised apathy than anything. I didn't want to return home. Why couldn't Sasha's family adopt me? I could be a much better son than Geoff could ever be, and Sasha's parents could be much better parents than Mom could ever be. Also, Jayden Serrano had a much better ring to it than Jayden Pico and especially better than Jayden Derry.

But I'd be eighteen in February, so there was that.

I took the last bite of my chile relleno and savored the cheese-stuffed green pepper while everyone else laughed softly at an embarrassing moment of Geoff's new American life.

"You'll be fine," Sasha said with an amused smile. "It just takes time."

"I know," he said with an overjoyed expression on his face. "The customs are different, and I must learn more because I didn't knew much things." He also raved about trying root beer with whipped cream and candy sprinkles, a drink that had quickly captivated him shortly after coming here, along with root beer floats, soda floats, ice cream sodas, and cream sodas of all kinds. He looked too comfortable like the new prince he didn't deserve to be.

I suppressed the urge to roll my eyes at the fact that I was no longer the center of attention during family dinners at Sasha's house. Why did Geoff have to be so greedy and steal all the attention? I felt completely invisible and suddenly got up from my seat. "I'm going to the bathroom right quick."

The others nodded me off, barely paying attention to whatever I said, since Geoff continued rambling on and on about life in Germany in comparison to life in the U.S.

Whatever.

I rolled my eyes on the way to the bathroom. After flushing the toilet and washing my hands, I looked through the mirror above the sink, tightly pressing my lips together as soon as my eyes glistened. Mom never cared about anything other than her prominent nightlife, and she couldn't even have the responsibility not to be late for work as often as she was, especially for being the only afternoon clerk at the general store.

Sasha's parents had come from Mexico, but all three daughters were born and raised in mainland Michigan before moving to Lac du Pac Island. Each of them was a year apart. Their hardworking parents had eventually become American citizens and made good money. They truly lived happily ever after like in fairytales, or so it seemed.

Mom and I kept to ourselves. I did my own thing, while

she partied and brought new man after new man home almost every night, mostly from mainland Michigan. One of them had seemed questionably interested in getting to know me "more personally" as he'd so put it, especially whenever he'd stroked my hair and caressed my shoulders with a creepy smile. *Ew…*I was *so* glad Mom had kicked him to the curb (though for other reasons). Only Sasha knew about the creepiness.

I couldn't remember the last time Mom and I had had an actual conversation, and Dad could stay gone after three years now. While Sasha was the only one who knew the truth about my family situation, it wasn't easy to control the cry for help. Sometimes, I needed to vent to someone else.

Ollie would be the perfect "someone else" if we could just continue being friends. I barely saw him at school, more like the occasional glimpse between classes, and all we could do was glance at each other with the kind of longingness I was sure we both felt and not just me. I needed him, and my crush on him didn't help at all.

Ugh, why couldn't Gracie have just butted out and left us alone? Well, she'd left *me* alone and pretended I didn't exist anymore, but *after* the fact. Ollie and I had been just fine without her, and his parents hadn't known anything to try to stop us from hanging out. We could've been closer than ever by now.

After my eyes flooded some more, I broke into quiet sobs at the memories of everything in my life. First Dad, then Mom, then Ollie…and I had to deal with Geoff taking Sasha away from me.

I couldn't take it anymore!

My phone chimed with a new text notification. I grabbed it and checked the screen. My eyes widened, and I wiped the tears off my face, sniffling a few times. It was the secret lesbian! I'd only heard from her the one time, and it was great to hear from her again. In her text, she apologized for the delay and asked if we could be friends. I quickly replied with my acceptance, and I hoped I could see her in person someday. But given her internalized homophobia, I didn't expect it to happen anytime soon, if ever.

Still, it was nice to hear from her. Maybe we'd keep in touch. I really needed a new friend, even if just through texting. I loved Sasha, but she'd been too busy with school and Geoff, and since she no longer offered me to come over like she usually did, I'd taken it as a sign that I was slowly fading away from her life.

As much as it killed me to accept it.

Chapter 7

On Tuesday morning, I sat in Principal Olsen's office. My new froggy backpack leaned against one of the legs of my chair, and instead of having a good day because of getting to use it, *this* had to happen.

She and I were having a serious discussion about my new T-shirt that read, *Was That Your Boyfriend in My Bed? I Thought He Looked Familiar!* What was so graphic about it? It was just a shirt. It wasn't racist or homophobic or anything like the *one* attention seeker a while ago who questionably hadn't been sent home right away like he should've been.

"Jayden, I just don't understand why you continue to test our dress code," Principal Olsen said in a defeated but stern tone, her face red. "You keep forgetting that there are young children in this building, not just high school students, and that shirt is still not appropriate. It's like you don't *think*. You think you can just wear whatever you like with no consequences? I'm sorry, but I'm going to have to send you home *again*." She shook her head.

I got up from my seat. "Are we done now? I get your point already." I tried hard not to snap.

"*Do* you, though? I honestly question whether you do."

I sighed. "I get it."

"Good. Then, yes, we're done. And this is your final warning. I'm not giving you another chance. You do this again, and you're getting suspended indefinitely. You do it once more after that, and I'll have to have a meeting with your mother for a possible expulsion."

Ugh, it was *not* that serious!

Principal Olsen circled around her desk and shoved a blue sweatshirt with the school's logo into my arms.

Drawing a big breath, I pulled the sweatshirt over my head and onto my torso, all while she waited to make sure I'd do so. It was baggy on me, not to mention ugly, instantly killing my mood. "Happy now?"

"*Watch* your tone, Jayden. Look, if you want to wear 'Rainbow Brite' or 'My Little Pony' shirts, knock yourself out, but *not* those kinds of shirts."

I rolled my eyes. "Fine," I muttered. "Can I leave now?"

"Yes, you may leave."

I grabbed my backpack and walked out into the hallway. I ignored the few snickers aimed at me, including from the annoying middle school kids. Whatever. They were probably jealous of my fabulous froggy backpack, which was more of an accessory because of its impractical small size, but it was cuter than the boring one I still had to lug around. I hated that I was a dude who was expected to wear what I didn't always want to wear. Just because I identified as male and used masculine pronouns didn't mean I had to uphold a masculine gender expression.

I stopped at my locker and sighed. Sometimes, putting up a front and telling myself not to care was tedious when I knew that, no matter what happened, the scrutiny would never end. I had to continue forcing myself not to care instead of telling myself I didn't. I had to feel the hate vanish and never come back. Most times, I didn't really care *as* much, but when it got to the point where I was confronted about it, that was when I had no choice but to deal with the drama.

My phone chimed with a new text notification, and I checked it to see that it was the secret lesbian. Her message about thanking me for our chats made me smile. We'd texted a few times almost every day. I wasn't sure if we were exactly friends because we hadn't established that yet, but we connected somehow. I still didn't know much about her, not even what grade she was in, and I imagined she wanted to keep it that way out of fear of being easily suspected in this tiny school. I'd suggested using a fake name, but for some strange reason, she didn't want one. Oh, well. Maybe we'd eventually meet in person after she felt comfortable enough.

Then again, maybe not.

I entered the school cafeteria during lunch period, still carrying my froggy backpack. A weak smile spanned my lips at Sasha chatting away with Geoff at our usual table, already with their food trays. They giggled while browsing through something that looked like yet another catalog. Ugh, why didn't they just get married already?

I pursed my lips and headed to the table with my food tray. I wished I could sit alone instead of feeling like the third wheel again, just like every day since Geoff had come to the island. Unfortunately, sitting alone would mean possibly being bullied again, unless Sasha still cared enough to save me for the nth time. Just sitting with her at the same table made me feel safe.

Geoff immediately noticed me. He lifted his glasses from sliding and formed his typical overjoyed expression. "Hi, buddy!" Ugh, we weren't *buddies*. He was getting *way* too comfortable as a foreign exchange student, and he needed to be shipped back to Germany. Why did Sasha's family have to be his host family in the first place?

Whenever I looked at him, despite his attractive face, it was with pure annoyance. I sat down and immediately stuffed my mouth with a corndog.

"We're looking at other colleges." Sasha had the widest smile, barely taking her eyes off what looked like a catalog in a different language. She tucked her curls behind her ears every so often.

Geoff continued looking and pointed at a picture after Sasha turned the page. "That's the student center. When I've gone on the tour, there were much things to do and much places also."

"It's so nice." Sasha made an impressed face. "That's it, I'm officially wowed."

"Yah, I really much like this university."

Why was it challenging to be a part of that? Was I

slowly being replaced? I didn't want to believe it, but the longer I was around the two of them, the more it made me feel this way. I couldn't help it, and while I hoped it would go away, I knew better than to believe it would. I hated this feeling. I wished I could join them more easily.

I swallowed another bite of my corndog, making an attempt to join them. "What school is that?" My voice was still weakish, though, but I'd tried.

"It's a university that I want to go," Geoff said, flashing his clenched teeth in sheer excitement. "It's in Germany, and it's a big campus with—"

"I was asking *Sasha*, not *you*." My tone couldn't have snapped any harder. I tried to control myself.

Geoff made an awkward face, his eyes hinting he was hurt with how they glistened. He resumed looking at the catalog without saying another word, his face reddening a little.

Well, *that* made me feel good. Maybe I shouldn't have talked to him like that. I felt a twinge of guilt, but I knew myself all too well. As soon as I got upset or defensive, I couldn't hide it.

Sasha looked up at me and raised an eyebrow. "Is...everything okay?"

"Yep." I gave her a curt nod and a tight smile, not bold enough to bring it up and possibly be seen as the villain of the group. Okay, maybe not to *that* extent, but I didn't want my mood to rain on their happy little parade.

"O-kay..." Sasha gave me one more glance as if to be sure, then focused back on the catalog and flipped another page. "Ooh, now *that's* nice." She was way too absorbed by the catalog.

Geoff finally made a little smile, but he wasn't as enthusiastic as before. "Yah, it is." He suddenly seemed a bit more reserved, maybe cautious. Great. He probably felt like I'd snap at him again.

"I'd love to go to Germany for at least a week or two, maybe even a month."

Geoff strengthened his expression, but it still wasn't back to how it'd been before I'd snapped at him. "You can go one day if you would like it."

"Oh, my parents would be fine with it, and they'd most likely buy me a ticket as long as one of my sisters join me so that I'm not alone. It's really just a matter of when."

I couldn't take it anymore. I began to lose my appetite, and the two new lovebirds deserved each other. Not once had I had some alone time with Sasha since Geoff had come into the picture, simply because he'd *had* to tag along. She hadn't noticed my cute froggy backpack the entire time I'd been here! Even the secret lesbian knew about it and had thought it sounded awesome.

Ugh, if only the leech could disappear forever!

Okay, maybe that was a bit mean. I had to calm down. I didn't want to be a terrible person. I just hated the feeling of not being able to connect with the two of them. I was able to connect with Sasha so naturally, and when Ollie had been with us, nothing had changed. Why was it different with Geoff when he'd been nothing but friendly to me? Maybe because Ollie had never been a threat and Geoff was. Ollie had never felt like a replacement, but more like an addition, like an added bonus to my friendship with Sasha. Not Geoff, though. I wanted him gone.

Could I make it happen?

Chapter 8

It was Thursday morning. By now, I lost track with how many times the annoying bond between Sasha and Geoff caused my eyes to roll with little effort. With my froggy backpack over my shoulders, I waited for her at her locker while she got ready for our next class. Why couldn't things have been the way they'd been when it'd been just the two of us? Or even with Ollie as our natural third if he'd been allowed to join us?

Geoff giggled, expressing an overjoyed mood. "You're so very funny, Sasha! Why you tell me always about those crazy stories? Or you make those crazy things with the head?"

She let out a titter. "I'm *not* making them up. Personal stories on gossip columns can be embarrassing. That's kind of the point and why they're so popular."

"Yah, it's because they're funny, and I laugh always."

I tried hard not to yawn.

"Sometimes, people do stupid things," Sasha added. "And this story was no exception. There are *tons* of embarrassing stories out there you can read."

More jokes and giggles between them, with Geoff looking more comfortable than ever. He was the star now, my replacement, the "brother" Sasha had always wanted because, in the end, he was more awesome than *I* ever could be.

Sasha sighed as if gasping for air, her face red from laughter. "You're so awesome, Geoff. I'm glad we met. It's too bad you can't stay here longer."

His eyes sparkled with joy. "Same! We spend time always together like a true duo."

"Aw, that's so sweet!"

Huh? A *true* duo? I looked at him with the deepest form of contempt, then gently bit my lower lip, readying myself. I let out a deep sigh as soon as I felt prepared to unload. "Ugh, I can't take this anymore!" Whoops, I'd raised my voice more than I'd expected to.

Sasha and Geoff were instantly mute, giving me awkward looks.

I tried to calm down, but I knew it was pointless. I narrowed my eyes at Geoff. "Ever since *you* came into this country, I haven't had the chance to spend any more time with my *best* friend the way I used to. It's like you took her away from me and got to have her *all* to yourself like an intruder."

Geoff was speechless, but his face spoke louder from what was probably a crack in his heart. He swallowed but remained mute.

Sasha's eyes were ready to pop out of their sockets. "Wow…" she said under her breath.

"I just don't get why you even came here," I added.

"Maybe you should just go back to *your* country and *stay* over there. Like, you know, *scram*."

"Jayden, oh my god, what's going on with you?" Unfortunately, Sasha didn't seem too pleased. The complete opposite. "Seriously?"

The more I'd spoken my mind, the more I realized I might've made things worse. How could I have let the jealousy get the best of me? I suddenly felt like a mean jerk.

Geoff tried to mask a frown, but his emotions didn't seem to allow that. "I'm so very sorry to break your friendship." His voice almost cracked. "I don't want to do that. I want only to experience the life in America and make good friends. I leave you now alone." With pain in his misty eyes, he didn't even part ways with Sasha before walking away from us and into the small hallway crowd.

Sasha narrowed her eyes, and the fury in her mood made me nervous.

I lowered my head, and a wave of guilt hit me harder than I'd been ready for. "Sash...I...think I messed up big time."

"You *think*?" She shook her head with a reddened face, except not from laughter. "You were like a diva on crack. That was *not* cool. It was actually mean, and you sounded *disturbingly* xenophobic." She rolled her eyes, shut her locker hard, and immediately walked away.

"Sasha, wait!" I desperately followed her. "I'm sorry!"

"Nope, I'm *so* not talking to you right now. You pissed me off with that nasty Karen attitude. Bye!" She waved at me in a way that looked more like swatting a fly, and she walked more rapidly until she was much farther ahead.

I stopped in the middle of the crowd. I couldn't even form a triumphant smile on my face for finally succeeding in chasing Geoff away. It smelled like the failure of a last-minute plan to take things back to the way they'd once been before he'd become an intrusion.

Except he wasn't an intrusion. He'd wanted to make friends just like I'd wanted to when I'd entered a whole new world that was known as high school just three years ago, even though it'd been in the same building as the other grades. He deserved to be treated with respect, and I'd ruined his American experience. I knew in my heart that I wasn't a xenophobic Karen, and while it sucked to be called that, I could suddenly see how my angry words had come off that way.

Now, I felt like the meanest idiot on the planet. How could I begin to apologize for how I'd acted? I'd said some mean things, and I really hadn't meant to go *that* far with speaking my mind. What had gone wrong with me! How could I have let myself take things too far out of desperation? In the end, I'd hurt Geoff badly, and I felt terrible about it. His eyes, his frown, his voice…all from the pain I'd caused.

With a deep frown, I turned around the other direction to hide in the bathroom for a moment until I accidentally bumped into someone. My eyes widened. "Ollie!"

He stopped walking and stood there, giving me a weak smile. "Jayden, hi." His tone was weak.

My heart melted from the sight of his face, his eyes locking with mine. How could my feelings for him go away when they lingered, especially whenever I saw him? Why couldn't people leave us alone and let our friendship be?

"I miss you," I said in a small voice, the pain striking me already. "Do you miss me too?"

He heaved a big breath. "I do, yes," he said in a lower tone. "Of course. I miss you *so* m—"

Gracie showed up right behind him in her exaggerated stomps, and she dramatically cleared her throat. I hadn't noticed her until now. Of course. She was most likely the hawk in his school life; he already had two hawks at home. He was probably on constant watch because *I* couldn't be trusted with my "bad" influence. Whatever. It was more like a bad dream, and I wanted to wake up and have everything be normal again.

Gracie didn't look at me, and while she pretended I didn't exist, I could tell she noticed me. My existence continued to offend her, and she wouldn't know kindness if it slapped her hard in the face, stars and all. "Ollie, we're going to be late for class. We don't want to fail any of our classes and not graduate, and I'm sure you don't want to get in trouble by your parents and risk failing them, since you're their good son." It wasn't an unfriendly tone, more like controlling through the power of passive aggression.

What a mean soul. Then again, I'd been just as mean myself a moment ago by hurting Geoff's feelings and making Sasha mad as a result. I had no room to talk.

Ollie gave Gracie a curt nod and barely glanced at me. "Jayden, you take care, okay?"

"You too." I watched as Ollie walked away, and my heart couldn't stop sinking. I missed him so much, and the fact that I still had a crush on him made it even worse. At least, he missed me a lot, and it made me feel special to know that. I hadn't doubted it, but I'd needed to hear it.

I wanted him to escape the island and take me with him. We could go to mainland Michigan and never come back, maybe live in a cute little cabin in the woods where no one could bother us. Okay, that was *obviously* a dream-come-false in a painfully cheesy cottagecore sort of way, but I wished so hard that I could at least spend more time with him. The occasional hallway glimpse was more like torture than anything, like the teaser for a canceled TV show. I needed more of him.

I continued toward the bathroom, willing to be a little late for class to give myself time to be alone and think about stuff. Had I lost Sasha too? She was the most important one to me, and I'd been so stupidly jealous that I could've very well destroyed what we'd had. I hoped not, though. I didn't want to lose her over my pettiness. I technically wasn't friendless, since I still kept in touch with the secret lesbian, albeit through texting, but Sasha and Ollie were more important because they'd been my actual friends. I had to find a way to get Sasha back because I didn't want to lose her.

I had to fix what I'd broken.

Chapter 9

By Friday, I'd had more than enough time to think things through. The rest of yesterday and all of this morning, I hadn't received a single acknowledgement of my existence, at least not from Sasha. She'd ignored my texts, so I'd been back to being on my own again for however long it lasted, and it drove me nuts. The thing was, it had all been my fault for not giving Geoff a chance. He'd only be here for *one* semester, a total of four months, and while I'd have the second semester of senior year to spend more time with Sasha, I'd also only have a half year with her in total before she'd move far away for college.

And I wasn't ready to lose her.

With my froggy backpack over my shoulders, I carried my food tray through the school cafeteria and marched toward our table. I knew I had to apologize and try to welcome Geoff the way Sasha already had. I didn't know him, didn't know much of what he liked, if anything. I had no choice but to accept him as part of the group after seeing just how happy Sasha seemed around him. In reality, she wasn't any less happy around me. I was just jealous and wanted her all to myself like the selfish idiot I continually felt I was.

And that wasn't fair to either of them.

I inhaled and let out my deepest breath as I reached the table and took a seat. They ended their chat as soon as they looked at me and became silent in that awkward sort of way, like I was bold to show up only a day after our drama. "Okay, look, I know I'm the *last* person you guys want to see right now. But I *really* have to apologize at the very least. I was a major idiot, and I was mean for no reason."

Geoff lifted his glasses from sliding and barely looked at me, still silent. I couldn't tell if he was upset, annoyed, sad, or all of the above. I'd hurt him, though, and it made me feel terrible. He didn't deserve to be treated like that— no one did.

Sasha finally let out a gentle sigh. "You were starting to act a little possessive, Jaydles. No offense." *Jaydles?* So, she wasn't angry with me anymore? She'd never call me that when mad. And possessive? Really? Wow, I hadn't seen it that way. It sucked to hear that, but I deserved it.

I looked at the two of them for a moment. Then, I focused more on Geoff. "I felt like you were a threat to my friendship with Sasha."

Geoff finally gave me his undivided attention.

I pursed my lips and swallowed. "Like, I was jealous because I felt left out every time we hung out." I looked back at Sasha. "We've been best friends for three years now. I felt like things were changing between us. Like you were replacing me with Geoff." My voice cracked, and I knew the emotions were coming their way. "I didn't know how to deal with that. And then with the fact that you're moving to Texas for college in less than a year. I got desperate."

She lowered her eyebrows. "So...you thought by chasing him away, things would be back to normal. *That* makes sense."

I looked down at my food with a completely vanished appetite, my face flushing with shame. "I'm sorry. I really am."

"Oh, Jaydles, why didn't you tell me any of this *before*? How did *I* know you were feeling like that? If anything, I thought you were just upset about losing your friendship with Ollie, which made sense, so I wanted to give you some space."

I looked back at her with a shrug. "I don't know. I mean, *yeah*, I'm still hurt about that, but I didn't need space. Maybe it was because I saw how happy you were with Geoff. I felt like an old burden."

"Okay, *now* you're being dramatic. That is *not* true at all and it'll *never* be."

Geoff formed a smile of reassurance. "You have a special friendship with Sasha. I try never to break that. I hope, that me and you are friends with us also. But I didn't thought that you have liked me."

I smiled in return, but not strong enough. Did we even share any interests? If not, maybe something along the way could pop up. I'd just have to learn patience. I sighed as if suffocating. "Can we just start over, please? This is already awkward."

"Yah, okay. So, Sasha has told me that you like electronica music."

My eyes widened. "Ugh, I love it! Why, do you?"

There was that overjoyed expression that I hadn't seen since before the fight, and I hadn't realized until now how much I liked seeing it. "Yah! More than one half of all the musics on my handy is much subgenres of electronica."

"Awesome!" I lowered my eyebrows. "What's a handy, by the way?"

Sasha looked at me, smiling along with us. "I'm pretty sure he means his phone. But see? You *just* found out you guys have something in common. Because you actually *chose* to give Geoff a chance."

I chuckled. "Okay, okay, so I was a brat. Happy now?"

She formed a toothy grin. "A bratty little diva with a tiara if we must be specific, but yeah, I'm happy now." Geoff and I suddenly bonding over something she didn't particularly care for didn't seem to affect her the way *her* bonding with *him* had affected *me*. I had a lot to learn, after all.

I looked back at him. "I also listen to lots of pop. You like Emma Emmy?" I mentally crossed my fingers.

He grimaced. "I don't like her music. She's a typical popstar like the others."

I gasped in a melodramatic fashion. "How can you say that? She is *not* typical. She's *fabulous*. Okay, I don't know you anymore, you're officially unfriended. *Bye*."

Geoff looked confused.

"Oh my god, I'm kidding!" I chuckled. "But seriously, she's my *all*-time favorite artist. She's the best blonde in the world, just like in her one song. Me and Sasha would *literally* kiss the ground she walks on."

Sasha nodded, unashamed. "We totally would. She's *that* awesome and we're *that* animated over her existence."

"I don't listen to pop music," Geoff said. "I listen only to electronica and synthpop musics with deep lyrics."

I realized Geoff and I still had some things in common, and that was enough to get started. Even though he was straight, I still found him very attractive in an Ollie-esque sort of way. If he'd been into guys, and if Ollie was out of the picture, I'd definitely take an interest in him. He was just as kind as Ollie, too, and he didn't seem religious, which was a plus.

"By the way, Jaydles," Sasha said. "I've been meaning to tell you that I love your new backpack. It's *so* cute."

"Yah, it's so very cute indeed," Geoff added.

They finally noticed my froggy backpack, which made me smile. "Thanks."

"You want one day to message on the handy, Jayden?" Geoff asked, his overjoyed expression returning.

"Sure, okay, yeah, but...you mean by phone, right? Because my mom doesn't have an international plan for that, and the phone bill would end up being much higher."

"No, we chat with us on the app, and it's free to chat with voice and video also."

"Oh, that'd be great." I was glad Geoff wanted to connect with me more, and I hoped we could grow close one day.

"But please, don't discuss about the religions and the politics," Geoff added with a chuckle. "But the other topics, yah, we can discuss about those things with us."

"I'm not religious, so no worries there."

"Oh, Jaydles," Sasha said, "I'm so glad you gave him a chance. It really means a lot."

That made me feel touched, and anything I did that pleased her pleased me.

"Yah, thank you for the chance." God, Geoff was so adorable, and he suddenly made no effort to leave me with a smile. I could look at him for a long time and admire his beauty, but he was straight, and that would probably be kind of creepy.

I didn't want to be *that* guy.

"No problem," I said. "You know, you kind of remind me of someone I know. Sasha knows him too."

"Oh my god, you mean Ollie?" Sasha asked, tittering. "He *does* kind of look like him. I didn't even think about it until you pointed that out."

Geoff looked confused. "That's good or bad?"

I tried to mask a big smile at the thought of Ollie but failed. "It's good. He's really special to me. You just have a lot of the same features."

Geoff looked like he blushed a little. "That's a good compliment."

"Ollie's pretty awesome," Sasha said. "So, yeah, definitely a good compliment."

"Cool!" That at least made Geoff happy, and he was so adorable about it.

Attraction aside, I was glad to have given him a chance, and the fact that we got along well gave me hope. I'd never imagined I could feel like he'd become an important part of the group within just moments after that discovery. I'd been blinded by my petty jealousy that I'd overlooked just how well he fit in with us. He'd already made a good third, and it made me smile with happiness. I felt better than I'd thought I would by talking to him. In fact, after getting to know him a bit more, not only did I feel terrible and guilty for hurting him, but it was going to be a tad sad to see him leave and head back to Germany.

Chapter 10

On Sunday, I rode on a horse-drawn carriage with Sasha and Geoff. The horses galloped down the main gravel road that offered an open view of the vast Lake Huron on my right side and expensive lake houses on my left. It wasn't Geoff's first time on a carriage, since he'd ridden on one a couple of times during my recent "mean boy" phase, but it was the first time I got to ride with him. Gone were the warm days of the summer, now that the chilly fall had arrived. Thankfully, the carriages had covers. While we wore light jackets, I still didn't like it one bit because it meant winter would eventually come sooner than I'd been prepared for. Why couldn't it have been summer year-round?

"We've traveled to a old time in this island," Geoff said in an overjoyed tone, sitting on Sasha's right side while I sat on her left. An emotionally lit smile spread across his lips while he was deeply focused on the foreign scenery. Well, foreign to *him*. That made me smile harder than I'd imagined, and for the first time, I felt a tickle in my heart in relation to him. I'd always been aesthetically attracted to him in a general sense, but it was weird how good he made me feel being around him. It was different compared to the other times I'd hung out with him, and I couldn't explain why that was or *what* it was. Even his soft but deepish voice soothed me.

Sasha tittered. "It's all part of the charm of Lac du Pac Island, and it's why we get a boatload of tourists."

I nodded. "Yeah, *literally*, since you can only come here by ferry. Well, there's charter flights and private planes and whatnot, but the ferries are more common. Pretty much the standard, actually."

"Yep," Sasha said. "It takes less than twenty minutes to ride on a ferry too. We'll go somewhere in the mainland so we can show you other parts of Michigan. The southeast region is the most populated because of Detroit."

"Cool!" Geoff said.

"The tourists here are so animated over the fudge in particular too."

"God, yeah," I added. "Very famous."

"Yah, I really much like the yummy fudge." Geoff smiled while still scoping the environment. "I see much Victorian houses here also."

"Like mine," Sasha added.

"Yah, your house is nice and big. I really much like it, and it's comfortable also."

"Glad you like it. And you've been sleeping well in the guestroom, so that helps. Jayden can tell you. He sleeps like a king there." Sasha winked at me.

I gave them a weak smile, trying to ignore the disappointing reminder of not being able to sleep there anymore until New Year's Eve. I also didn't feel the need to show off about my house because there was nothing special about it. A small, two-bedroom cottage wasn't all that impressive, not to mention the few ugly shotgun shacks scattered throughout my road. Sasha's road was far more upscale with none of *those* kinds of houses.

As the driver turned toward a residential road, guiding us farther down, a tiny shack captured my attention with its pale-yellow siding and bright-green roof. I didn't remember that one. Was it new?

"Ohhh, look!" Geoff cooed while pointing. "That little house is so very cute!"

Sasha smiled warmly. "It actually does look kind of cute in a charming sort of way. I don't think I've seen that house before."

"Someone lives in there, you think?"

"Who knows?"

Ugh, were they kidding me? It was an eyesore and looked more like a kid's playhouse. It stuck out like a sore thumb, and it totally needed to be demolished. I kept my mouth shut, though.

As we rode even farther down, my eyes widened at the sight of Ollie walking alone. My mouth dropped open, and I suddenly wanted the driver to stop. I turned to my left side and waved. "Ollie!"

He quickly looked and stopped, giving me a little wave and a weak smile. What was he doing alone around here? Shouldn't he be at home where his parents would watch him more closely? Looking at him made me want to jump out of the carriage, but I could get fined for that, and Mom would be mad at me for having to pay a lot of money for my misbehavior.

As we rode past him, I couldn't hide my frown. I hated it so much that I couldn't get to see him whenever I wanted, not even text like we used to.

"Hey, Driver? Can we stop for a minute, please?" Why was Sasha calling for the driver's attention? She managed a little smile at me. "Go talk to Ollie. I know you want to."

I raised my eyebrows. "You sure?"

"Yeah, yeah, go ahead. Geoff and I will continue ahead with the rest of the tour. Besides, I know you don't normally get to see Ollie, so maybe this is your chance to figure something out."

Geoff looked away on the other side, probably minding his own business out of respect.

As soon as the driver slowed the horses down to a stop, my heart raced. I couldn't believe I'd see Ollie for longer than a glance. "Sash, I...I just..."

"I know, Jaydles. You like him a lot, and that's why I want you to be happy because you deserve it after what Kail did to you."

"I like him more than you know." I wanted to cry from the heavy emotions hitting me hard. "It's different than what I felt for Kail, Sasha. Like...I don't know how to explain it because I'm still so inexperienced with this stuff, but it's just different."

"I think you're falling in love with Ollie, aren't you?"

Was I? I didn't know about *that*, but I definitely believed it was stronger than I'd meant to feel. As much as I'd fallen for Kail before seeing his true colors, I'd still had doubts and sad moments about my unrequited feelings for him. With Ollie, while it might've been one-sided, it at least felt more real on my part, which made it even sadder because he was actually special. There wasn't the kind of desperation attached to my feelings like with Kail. Whatever it was with Ollie, I knew it was something I couldn't ignore. We were only supposed to be friends, but my crush on him continued to grow by the day. "I don't know what I feel. I just know it's strong."

Sasha sighed, smiling more. "Well, the driver's waiting now, so go. I'll keep Geoff company while you stay here with Ollie. I hope it works out with you two. Good luck, okay? And I want *all* the juicy details."

I gave her a touched expression in return, thanking her in silence. "Thanks, Sash! See you later, Geoff!"

He waved at me with a weak smile that seemed a bit forced, unlike his usual expressions. "Good lucks!" Even his voice sounded a bit weaker than normal.

I rushed out of the carriage and ran after Ollie who'd already continued walking. I ran so fast like my life depended on it, the carriage continuing its way from behind me. I was painfully out of breath by the time I reached closer to him, and he turned around to see me like the pathetic dork I was.

He formed a wide smile that showed the perfect, white teeth I'd longed to see because of that particular heartwarming expression. "Jayden, hi! You came after me!"

I caught my breath, painful as it was to have run only a short distance because of how fast I'd moved, given that I was unfit. I gave him a rushed nod. "Ollie, look," I said breathily. "I know we're not supposed to be friends, but..." I caught some more air and swallowed. "But I want to figure something out. There *has* to be a way we can still keep in touch." I caught even more air. God, why had I run that fast!

"There might be, yes. But what could be a way? I can't think of any."

I tried my hardest to think of anything that popped into mind while catching the last of my breaths. I was able to relax more.

Ollie frowned a little. "Aw, Jayden, you shouldn't have run like that. You need to be careful, okay?"

The more I stared at him, the more I wanted to proclaim my crush on him right then and there. I felt such an urge to, like it was the right time. As I opened my mouth, I couldn't. What if it really was one-sided? Oh, God, I'd feel like the biggest fool on the planet.

"I'm not supposed to be out, actually, but after a big argument with my parents, I ran away."

My eyebrows flew up. "Wait, what? You ran away?"

He gave me a nod. "I did, yes. I told them that I felt like a prisoner and was getting very depressed. They insisted that maybe I needed to have a talk with a Christian counselor, and I told them that wasn't a solution. That made them really upset. You see, we're supposed to be leaving the island tomorrow for a special ministry that involves ex-gay conversion."

"Oh..." Wow, Ollie's parents were definitely quite the fanatics. I'd known it, but hearing stuff like that reminded me of just how so.

"Yes. My parents have done that kind of ministry before, plenty of times. It's usually out of state, but sometimes in the mainland. It's *so* uncomfortable whenever they drag me along with them. I don't take part in the ministry, but I'm still forced to attend and watch every single time. It's private, and no one else but you knows about it, not even the church members. I want *nothing* to do with any of that, so that's another reason I ran away."

"Ugh, I don't blame you." What a disgusting ministry that hurt more than it helped. Poor Ollie. He needed protection from those monsters. "But...you have school."

"They usually do it in the summer, but they sometimes do it when I have school. I don't like having to miss school for a whole week, especially for *that* reason."

I frowned. "Sucks."

"Yes. So. Here I am. I don't know where to go from here. I don't want to go back home, though."

I couldn't believe what I was about to suggest, but I couldn't help myself. "Stay at my house."

"Oh, I couldn't intrude like that, no. But thank you for the offer." He at least didn't seem uncomfortable about it, so that was good.

I grabbed onto his arm with a gentle grip. "Ollie..." Ugh, I couldn't say it.

"Jayden, that's the second time you've wanted to tell me something. I can tell by your expression. Why don't you just tell me?"

I looked away for a moment and sighed. "I can't," I said under my breath. "I *want* to, but...I just can't. I'm scared to tell you."

It took Ollie a moment to say something. "Jayden…I like you."

I looked at him until our eyes locked into a deep gaze. "I like you too. *So* much."

"So. Was that what you wanted to tell me? That you have feelings for me?"

Ollie's sudden question knocked the wind out of me, and I swore I could faint from the nervousness. Oh. My. God. How had he guessed? My breathing increased to heavy pants, and I was so afraid of our friendship being over because of my feelings making him uncomfortable. I couldn't even look at him while I acted like an idiot.

"Oh, great," Ollie said in a sad tone.

When I managed to take a glimpse of his face through the corner of my eye, I noticed he was looking at a carriage approaching us. I cast my eyes toward that direction and looked to see if I recognized any faces. Oh, great, indeed. His parents! No, no, no. Ugh, why?

And what a good thing that I wasn't wearing my froggy backpack today because they definitely would've thought it was super gay.

It was Ollie's turn to start panting, but less dramatically than me. "I guess this is goodbye, Jayden." His defeated voice broke me into bits, and I couldn't take it anymore. I was so sick of those people trying to come between us, all because Gracie had felt threatened by what Ollie and I had together. I'd run all the way here after him for a reason. I wasn't going to give up just like that. No, we'd stay friends, and I suddenly had the most uncomfortable idea that would certainly work like a charm. I didn't want to have to do it, but I was left with no choice if I wanted to be with him.

The carriage stopped near us, and Ollie's dad gave me the kind of angry stare that practically sent me to Hell. His wife had a similar one that was a bit milder, but I could tell she didn't like me at all. Neither of them did.

Still, I'd do it. I wouldn't back out. My bond with Ollie was hanging on a thread, and I needed to protect it. I refused to end it with him. There was no way he wasn't going to get in trouble and possibly be watched even more. What if he got sent away somewhere? I'd never forgive myself if something bad happened to him in relation to running away.

I rushed to his parents, and I gave them the most desperate expression I could fake, my eyes forcefully misty. I inhaled and exhaled, and I made sure my words sounded like a plea. "Hi, Mr. and Mrs. Belasco. Can I go to church with you and Ollie? I don't want to live in sin anymore. I want to be saved, and I'm scared that I'm going to go to Hell." What a terrible aftertaste those words left, and my mood sank like it was tied to an anchor, pulling it into the depths of sadness.

The things I did for a guy.

Their stunned faces gave me hope, though. They looked at each other like they couldn't believe what they'd just heard. From the corner of my eye, I could imagine Ollie was shocked too.

When his parents looked back at me, Mrs. Belasco smiled warmly, shocking me to my core. "Believe it or not, I prayed that this would happen."

Oh? They'd actually prayed for me? I didn't know what to say about *that*, but I knew I had to continue feigning whatever convincing tone I could. "Really?"

Even Mr. Belasco smiled a little when he nodded. "We both did. Every single day, and we asked our church members to pray for you too. We're not the scary *monsters* that the woke media wants you to believe."

I suddenly felt popular by accident, and not in a good way. It was a little creepy, if anything. Then again, I was convinced Gracie was the exception. There was *no* way she prayed for me, and if she did, it was for God's giant hand to fall from the sky and crush me like an ant. "I don't know what to say, but I'm touched."

Not.

"Well, we knew how much you mean to Ollie," Mrs. Belasco said.

They did? I couldn't believe their reaction because it was nothing like I'd ever expected. I'd been convinced that they'd looked at me as an unforgivable sinner who was a lost cause and unworthy of being saved.

I glanced at Ollie as briefly as possible to avoid any suspicion. He did seem touched, at least.

Mr. Belasco nodded. "So, we prayed in hopes that God would speak to you, to give Ollie the chance to have a pure friendship with you. After all, we want our son to be happy and safe."

I had to admit that that last part kind of touched me a tad, but not exactly in the way they'd meant it. It touched me because, regardless of how they looked at things, they thought I was special enough to be Ollie's friend.

"Now, just so you're aware," Mr. Belasco added, "we don't like your lifestyle because God doesn't like it, so whatever God doesn't approve of, we don't either."

Mrs. Belasco shook her head with an apologetic expression, agreeing with him. Then again, it was probably more of "sorry, not sorry" face. Not that I was surprised.

"But! If you're willing to change in order to be saved, we'd be more than happy to welcome you to Holy Light of Emmanuel." He gave me what seemed like a genuine smile. "I'm Pastor Belasco, by the way."

My eyes almost popped out at the revelation. Ollie had never mentioned his dad was an actual pastor. All that time? Then again, it wasn't like he'd lied because I'd never asked, and he knew I tried to avoid religion whenever we chatted. Now that I knew his dad was the pastor, it made sense why his life was a living religious hell.

I tightened my lips into whatever positive expression I could make. "I didn't know you were the pastor there."

"Oh, yes. Ten years now."

Mrs. Belasco formed a smile of pride. "He's a wonderful pastor, but of course, I'm his wife, so I may be biased."

The three of us laughed softly, me in the most uncomfortably contrived way.

"Well, it's nice to meet you," I said. "You know, Ollie told me what happened, but I convinced him to go back home because he needs to be with his family. I live with a single mother, so things aren't the greatest on my end. Maybe that's why I admire Ollie so much because he's such a good Christian with strong faith, and I can see that he takes after you two." Ugh, I suddenly felt weird saying all that.

Ollie's parents looked touched. Mrs. Belasco smiled again. "Thank you for your kind words, and thank you *so* much for talking Ollie into coming back home because he needs to be where he belongs. We're going to be out of town tomorrow for a private ministry. We'll be gone for a whole week, until the beginning of October. We're postponing all worship services and Bible studies until then, but when we come back, we'd love to see you in church."

So, Ollie really *was* stuck going to that toxic ministry. Ugh, if only I could save him from going with a convincing lie, but I couldn't afford to push my luck. I only hoped he'd survive it, even though it wouldn't be his first time going.

I forced a strong expression on my face. "I've never gone to church in my life because my parents aren't religious, so it'd be a new experience for me. It'd actually be an honor to serve God in His house." Okay, Jayden, shut up already! I couldn't risk overdoing it.

Mr. Belasco sighed with emotion. "Praise God! He woke something in you, and that's the only kind of *woke* I accept. He really does work in mysterious ways. And I have faith that He has a plan for you and that He's working with you. After all, you did God's first work, which was to bring Ollie back home. We're forever grateful for that. Thank you again."

"You're welcome." When I finally looked at Ollie again, his big smile melted me in ways I couldn't describe. He knew why I'd done it. He knew I wasn't serious about being saved when I wasn't even a believer myself. Then again, I wasn't sure if I was an atheist or not since I was more undecided than anything. Still, I got to see him whenever I wanted, on top of possibly reconnecting with him through texting, which meant his parents could finally trust us to hang out. I'd sacrificed what little social life I had just for him because he meant that much to me, because losing him was painful enough, because my crush on him drove me to make such a crazy and desperate decision. Plus, making him happy made *me* happy.

My crush on Ollie, though. It had almost slipped, and my silence might've given me away. When he'd asked me about my feelings for him, I realized he didn't sound uncomfortable. He sounded curious. Maybe he was flattered. Maybe he thought it was adorable.

Or maybe he was hopeful because he actually felt the same way.

Chapter 11

It was the first Tuesday of October. Ollie had come back from his parents' toxic ministry last night. What had they done for a whole week? Guilt gays and lesbians into a conversion that wasn't possible? Ugh.

I'd told Sasha and Geoff the same day I'd come up with the plan, and they'd been both excited and worried, especially Sasha. I'd insisted it'd be fine because it was impossible for me to be a serious member of Holy Light of Emmanuel, and they'd wished me the best. I hadn't told them about the ex-gay ministry, since Ollie had confided in me with that. I knew how they'd react, especially Sasha.

I left the school building and walked home, wishing I could wear my froggy backpack. If only it wouldn't bother Ollie's parents. I grabbed my phone after it chimed with a text notification, and I smiled at Ollie's affectionate message. I more than smiled, actually. I was giddy to hear from him, since he hadn't been able to contact me while he'd been away. His parents had finally given him his phone back, all because my plan had worked.

Apparently, he had something to talk to me about

soon, and it seemed serious. He'd been back in school today, but we'd only waved and smiled at each other because Gracie had apparently not gotten the memo that Ollie's parents were finally cool with me. Either that, or she'd refused to be nice for personal reasons.

Ugh, but church, and the thought of it made me groan. Later in the evening, it'd be my first time attending a service there, and I was convinced I'd be bored out of my mind. Oh, well. It was what I'd agreed to in order to keep ties with Ollie, so I had to suck it up. Yep, the things I did for a guy.

I got a new text from the secret lesbian telling me that she wished she could reveal herself but that she was too afraid. I quickly replied and told her there was no rush. I didn't want to add any more pressure than she already felt just by dealing with her sexuality. I hoped she'd continue to manage. We still texted each other periodically almost every day, and I always made sure to remind her that she wasn't alone in feeling how she did. I wanted to instill all the hope in her that I could so that she could know it was okay being a lesbian. Baby steps.

I entered the house, and Mom was sitting on the long couch in the living room with company. Next to her was a brunet with a long ponytail and a long goatee. Their eyes were glued to a reality show about giving makeovers to guests' old motorcycles. Empty beer cans were scattered across the coffee table, and a couple of them had rolled onto the floor.

Mom belted out a raspy chortle at a comment made by one of the show's guests, and the new man cackled along. She grabbed a cigarette and lit it, not caring that her dyed-blond hair looked like it had gone through a tornado. That only meant they'd done the deed in her room while I'd been at school. I was relieved about that because I didn't have to worry about hearing them.

I rolled my eyes and didn't feel the need to greet the new man. It wasn't like he'd last long, anyway. I gave it a couple of days, maybe a week. I walked directly into my room and set my things on the floor. I headed out to the kitchen as soon as my stomach grumbled. Scrambling through the cupboard, I found it difficult to stay home and put up with Male Guest Number...well...who was counting, anyway?

"Hey!" The volume of the man's deep and hoarse tone wasn't necessary when he'd called me all of a sudden. "Grab me a beer, will you?"

Mom was too absorbed by the show while blowing some smoke.

I scoffed, barely looking at him. "Grab it yourself."

"Well, you're near the fridge, are you not?" He formed a lopsided grin. "Marsha, can you grab me a beer?"

"I'll get it, I'll get it." Mom finally got up from the couch.

The man playfully slapped her butt with a growl while groping the front of his jeans for a brief moment.

That *really* made me cringe! *Ew...*

Mom giggled. "Not now, Mitch, my son's here."

He released a dramatic sigh. "All right, all right, I'll behave."

Mom entered the kitchen to grab a beer can from the fridge.

I studied Mitch for a moment. The stained, white tank top was full of cigarette ashes, and he didn't seem to care who was around before lifting his leg to let out a loud and long fart. He scratched his head furiously, briefly observing his fingernails before wiping them on his jeans.

I grimaced. "*Really*, Mom?"

"What are you now, the love expert? Don't worry about Mitch. He's *my* man, not yours. Besides. We've been dating for a month now, and I actually like him."

A month...?

"We actually met in January but didn't make it official until early last month. He's a keeper."

I arched an eyebrow. "A keeper?" Also, I must've not paid much attention to the men she'd brought home before because I definitely didn't remember seeing Mitch come over. She'd known him for almost a year now!

"*Yeah*, a keeper. Why not? He lives in the mainland, he has a trucking job that makes *really* good money, and he actually knows what he wants."

"But he looks like he's half your age." I couldn't even take her seriously. That said, I was a bit surprised they had lasted *that* long. But to say that Mitch actually knew what he wanted implied that Mom had wanted more than just sex all along.

"Hey, he treats me right, which is a *lot* more than I can say for most men I've hooked up with. And besides, he's almost thirty, not exactly a boy last time I checked. *Believe* me, I know."

My appetite vanished. Granted, Mitch was in great shape and would probably be decent-looking if he shaved his face and got a decent haircut, but that still didn't eliminate the fact that he was a slob with no manners. It was a sad discovery when it came to the men in Mom's life, especially because *that* one in particular just *had* to be the one to stay put, because of *course*. "Ugh, I'm taking a walk. Later."

"Bye." She seemed a bit sad, unlike usual, but who cared?

I reentered my room to grab my jacket and rushed back into the living room on my way to exit the house. All of a sudden, I tripped over Mitch's bulky work boot and fell forward onto the floor with a yelp.

"Oh, crap, sorry about that!"

I got up and faced him with narrowed eyes. "*Are* you? Or did you do that on purpose?"

Mitch looked extremely apologetic and shook his head quickly. "Honest to God, I swear I didn't. No hate here at all. I just want peace."

I studied his face more, and my heart raced. I tightened my mouth for a while. "Oh my god...you look...*really* familiar. And *not* in a good way."

Mitch paused, looking like he pondered something. Then, he sighed. "Guess I'm caught. Yep, I used to film adult videos as Big D Dixon, but I quit last year, no worries." His face reddened only slightly, but he controlled it.

Mom gasped lightly as she approached us, stifling a laugh. "Jayden, what were you doing watching porn?" *Her* face was definitely redder than Mitch's.

"*Mom*, it was, like, *one* time while I was browsing out

of boredom." Plus other times on occasion, only softcore stuff with just kissing and foreplay. I suddenly cringed at the memory of such a face I couldn't forget, and I definitely remembered that stage name. I was *so* relieved he hadn't been an actor I cared for at all. Otherwise, it would've been *really* awkward. I only remembered him because his preview clips had been everywhere in site ads, mostly MILF videos. "Busty and the Big Beast" starring Big D Dixon suddenly rang a bell.

Ew...

I shuddered and couldn't look at Mitch anymore, and I suddenly needed memory bleach. I rushed out of the house in need of some air. If only the temperature wasn't colder than a few weeks ago. Either way, I tried to put all of that out of my mind.

I remembered being a child when I'd wondered which of my parents would win the intense argument. Although no physical violence had occurred, the shouting words that had echoed across the house had proven undefeatable.

I remembered when Dad had said his final words before giving me one last kiss on the forehead and storming out of the house. The last goodbye had been just that, and it had caused Mom to let herself turn into her current self. Dad had simply been a coward who'd refused to give our family another chance, all because he'd no longer loved us. Otherwise, why would he have left? It was an experience that continued to make my blood boil.

I pressed my lips together tightly while breathing through my nostrils, and I blinked a few times to lessen the wateriness of my eyes. I exhaled and continued near the entrance to Lac du Pac Island State Park. I chose the first swing I saw, barely anyone around. I sat slumped with a droopy face, and I needed to talk to someone. Sasha was busy with homework and studying, but I decided to send her a quick text about Mitch and who he was, so I grabbed my phone from my jeans pocket and vented. She replied with a sad face.

I now hoped Ollie was free. Even though I'd see him in church later, I probably wouldn't have time to talk to him like normal. I called him instead of texting.

After the fourth ring, he finally answered. "Jayden, hi. God bless you." Okay, he hadn't said *that* since the ninth grade, so his parents must've been around. His tone also sounded like there was caution, so, most likely. I imagined he'd always be careful just to be safe. Would they still act like hawks even though we were allowed to be friends again?

Ugh, I hoped not.

"Hey." I didn't know what to say anymore. I'd been ready to talk like normal, but with his parents possibly there, what exactly could I talk about?

"So. Are you ready for church tonight?"

Definitely not, but I knew better than not to fake it. "As ready as I'll ever be."

"Good, good."

"I'm sure it'll be an interesting experience, right?"

"It will be, yes. I'm especially curious about how it'll make you feel."

Sometimes, it was hard to tell whether Ollie was actually happy about me going to church or if he was just happy that he got to see me, or both. "I'm sure I'll see things in a different light."

"You just might, yes. You have to have faith. It might not seem easy at first, but you'll start to feel it when you let it come to you."

Things were getting a little uncomfortable already, and I hoped Ollie was just playing along with that kind of talk. So much for wanting to chat in private. At the same time, it was nice hearing his deep voice. I'd come up with a great plan to keep my friendship with him alive.

I wanted more, though.

Chapter 12

It was evening, and I let out a silent groan while standing in front of Holy Light of Emmanuel. It was a tiny brick cathedral with several stained-glass windows on both sides and a wooden double door that looked medievalesque. It had to have cost a fortune to build, given the uncommon architecture on the island, and it wasn't even the main church here. It was pretty to look at, though.

I opened the right side of the doors and trudged inside the brightly lit sanctuary, masking a frown that was itching to form. A few members sat silently in the wooden pews on each side, and they turned their heads toward me and greeted me with polite smiles. I put on my tightest smile as a response, feeling more uncomfortable than anything. I was at least a little early, which was good. It would've been worse had I come here while the service started.

The interior was simpler than I'd imagined it to be, given the exterior. White walls, red carpet, and a high ceiling. A wooden podium was centered at the altar with a huge golden-colored cross serving as the backdrop. There was a door on either side of the altar, but since they were closed, I didn't know where they led. I looked behind me to my right, and there was a stairway to the basement. I turned to my left and noticed a stairway there too. What an interesting design.

There were others kneeling in front of the pews while resting their elbows on the seating, praying with devotion. I'd signed up for this. It'd been so easy to do it at the time, but reality hit me now. I'd be here every week on Tuesday and Thursday evenings, and Sunday mornings, for two hours each time, and for months to come.

Or years?

One of the praying members stood up from her knees, and it was Gracie. Her face was priceless. She totally didn't expect to see me here. She looked like she wanted to smile but kept her reservation, instead. Maybe she wondered what I was up to after daring to cross her territory. She didn't say a single word to me, and she turned around and took a seat. That figured, and I wasn't surprised.

Ugh, whatever.

"Jayden, hi!" a familiar voice whispered from behind.

I turned around and spied Ollie at the top of the left stairway, and with a big smile, he wiggled his fingers for me to follow him downstairs.

I glanced back at Gracie who had already looked our way while she was still seated, her face reddening. She had the face of a hawk as if making sure I wasn't up to no good. Well, she could go to Hell, for all I cared.

I finally followed Ollie down the creaky stairway that curved to face the same direction as the altar was upstairs. The basement was finished with concrete block walls that were painted white, a gray floor that was polished, drywall ceiling tiles that looked new, gendered bathrooms on either side straight ahead, and a kitchenette centered upfront. With a banquet table in the center of the basement, I imagined the members held plenty of dinners here.

"So. What do you think?" Ollie asked. We had to speak in a low tone because our voices could probably travel through the silence upstairs.

Despite having to lower our voices, there was at least no one down here to hear us directly, so I felt safe to speak my mind. It was a good thing that going down the stairs made enough noise to become alert because of the creaky steps.

"It looks nice here," I said. "But, you know, it's a *church*."

"It is, yes. I know. Thank you for what you did, though. I didn't expect that at all."

I strengthened my expression a little because it was Ollie, and he had that effect on me every time. "Well? I guess I'll do anything for you, right? Do you think I'm an idiot?"

"I don't, no. Not at all." He took my hands and pulled me toward him. Then, he wrapped his arms around me for a tight embrace, letting out a gentle moan of affection. "Jayden, I can't thank you enough. I'll make it up to you."

I faced him while still in his arms, melting as his eyes peered into mine. "You don't have to, Ollie. I did it because I couldn't stand not being able to see you again. I'll never, ever be a serious member here, but I'll continue to go when I can if it means I get to have you back in my life."

He didn't say anything else, but his expression spoke enough. He was touched; I felt it. We were so comfortable with each other that we could hug like this, look into each other's eyes, and be sweet with each other without a lot of awkwardness. In fact, the awkwardness had faded away the more we did these things.

Ollie did something he'd never done before. He rested his forehead against mine, his gaze locked with mine, and this particular affection sped up my heartrate. "Jayden...I'd like to believe you have romantic feelings for me. It just seems so clear to me, but I need a confirmation. I need to know the truth. Do you...have those kinds of feelings for me?"

I froze, my heart pounding and my body trembling. *That* question again. I'd been able to avoid it when his parents had found us on the road, but I couldn't avoid it a second time unless someone came downstairs. "Ollie, I...um..."

"Whatever the answer is, I won't be uncomfortable around you. I promise." He seemed truthful about it, at least. I knew when he was comfortable or not, after all.

I couldn't stop studying every detail of his face, every reaction from it. My eyes grew heavy with the romance version of horny, whatever the word was. What most guys felt in their penises, I felt in my heart, and *only* in my heart. My body couldn't respond the way Ollie's probably did. I wasn't sure how exactly he felt, but I didn't want to turn him on again. His expression gave me hope that he wasn't focused on that.

"Jayden, please tell me. You do, don't you?"

Why couldn't I say it? Why did I have to be so stupid about it every time? The truth was that I did have feelings for him, and strong ones, at that. I didn't know what to call it except for a crush, but it often felt stronger than that. What I'd started feeling for him before school had started was a smaller version, definitely a crush then. I was convinced it was no longer that. Maybe Sasha was right.

Maybe I was in love.

Our faces leaned closer until our lips were just an inch apart. Ollie's warm breath tickled my lips, and for the first time, I actually wanted him to kiss me. I hadn't really thought much about kissing when it came to him, mostly cuddling and holding hands, but right now, I did. I wanted nothing more than to feel his lips on mine, no tongue necessary. I just wanted a simple but special kiss that I'd never do with anyone else.

The corners of Ollie's mouth drooped a bit. "If you don't have feelings for me, it's not a real biggie. I'll understand, and I won't be mad about it. But I also know that friends don't act the way we sometimes do, like right now."

I gave him a weak nod. He was right. Friends didn't act the way we did. We didn't always act like friends. We sometimes acted more like in a label-less sort of way. I couldn't stall anymore. I needed to dip my feet into the pool of love, toes first. At this rate, it was clear it wasn't one-sided, so it made no sense to keep avoiding the truth. "I like you, Ollie."

Just one corner of his mouth rose. "I like you, too, but you already knew that."

One foot in. "But, I…*like*…you."

"I *like* you too."

Both feet dipped, and my heart was ready to burst out of my chest. "I'm…in love with you." Oh, my god. Oh, my god! I'd said it! I'd *actually* said it.

Ollie's lips curled into a wide smile. "Jayden," he said breathily. "That was what I needed to hear. It's what I've waited to hear this whole time. Because I've been in love with you since middle school."

My jaw was ready to drop, and I definitely hadn't expected *that* admission. Ollie had been in love with me the entire time? *All* these years? Even when he'd first talked to me in the boys' bathroom on our first day of high school? Oh. My. God. My lips mimicked his, and I found myself burying my face in his chest. Looking at him had suddenly made me way too shy.

He rubbed my back for a moment, and he got me to look at him again, the two of us smiling like dorks in love. "Jayden, I want to kiss you, but not in church."

Wow, to know we could finally share a kiss really made me melt. My dream had finally come true, to find a guy who'd actually feel the same way as I did when it came to love. He had a point, though. While I didn't see it the same way he did, I wanted to respect his views since he respected mine. "I get it, and I respect your decision."

"Thank you. I really appreciate that. I just don't feel right about doing that here, not even a chaste kiss. It's very disrespectful to do that in the house of the Lord."

"I get it, Ollie, I do."

"Good, good." He couldn't stop smiling. "So. Now that

we got that out of the way, what does it make us? What are we?"

"You mean…a title?"

"A title, yes."

What *were* we? We definitely weren't platonic friends anymore because we'd crossed a whole new bridge that platonic friends never crossed. At the same time, we hadn't gone out on a date yet. To even get this far with a guy for the first time was a milestone in and of itself. Kail had been the only other guy I'd gotten involved with, and he hadn't loved me back. Then again, I wasn't sure if it'd been love on my part to begin with. I'd felt like it could've been, but at the same time, not quite. With Ollie, though, it definitely was, or *close* to it, anyway.

"Should we go on a date first?" I wasn't sure how this dating thing even worked.

"We could do that, yes. But is it necessary to wait until then for a title?"

"Probably not. I mean, I'm not against calling you my boyfriend."

"I'm not, either. I guess we kind of already are boyfriends, right?"

"Yeah." My first boyfriend, and in the most ironic location. That was okay, though. What mattered was that the dance between us that had led up to being boyfriends was over. We were finally together.

The way we were meant to be.

Chapter 13

On Friday evening, I rolled my eyes at the sight of Mitch. He sat in the living room, watching a wrestling match. I'd recently learned his last name was Hunt, the first time Mom had dated someone whose last name I got to know, not that it was big deal to me.

Mom was in the shower, getting ready for a night with him of barhopping on the island. I couldn't remember the last time it was when she'd done that since she usually partied at home. Of all men, *this* one had lasted long enough to start becoming relevant in a way I couldn't ignore, and I wasn't sure how I felt about it. Did I even need a stepdad? *Was* it that serious?

Mitch burped loud enough to startle me, and he scratched his head. He glanced at his fingernails and wiped them on his stained, white tank top that looked questionably worn. "I need a shower *bad*. I'll shower after your mom gets out. I wanted to shower with her, but I wasn't sure how you felt about us showering together."

Why was Mitch talking about that? I didn't want to

hear any of it. I couldn't care less if they showered together as long as I didn't hear anything my ears didn't need to hear.

He took the last sip of his beer can before treating the floor as a trashcan, more like dropping it than actually throwing it.

I felt a strong need to clean up after him to avoid more pests. He probably made much more money than Mom did for much harder work, being a trucker and all, but we weren't his maids.

He smiled at me, a bit loopy from however many beers he'd already had. "Jayden, right?"

I wasn't in the mood to chat with Mitch, and it was easy to feel annoyed by his presence. Why couldn't he just leave already?

He chuckled. "You don't like me very much, do you?"

"I never said that." I didn't care if I snapped at him. I was under no obligation to be friendly.

"You don't have to. It's obvious." Why was he so calm, though? He couldn't have been *that* drunk from what I'd just counted as only three beer cans. Shouldn't he be annoyed, at the very least? Oh, who cared! Fathers were worthless, anyway, and potential stepfathers even more so.

I remained silent while I continued cleaning up the living room after him.

"I do like your mother, just so you know. I know you probably don't believe it."

I failed to understand why Mom had even bothered with such a gross swine. Was she really *that* desperate for the company of a man? Why couldn't she just grow up, get her independence back, and be the mother she was supposed to be?

Mitch chuckled again. "Come on, son. Talk to me. What are your hobbies? What do you like to do for fun?"

I stopped abruptly with a raised eyebrow. My eyes glared at his direction. "I'm *not* your son."

He shrugged but didn't seem hurt. "Just trying to be nice. My mistake."

I rolled my eyes and couldn't continue cleaning up anymore. I marched into my room to grab my jacket, and I stormed out of the house, slamming the front door. The temperature continued warning me of what would soon come. If only summer hadn't come and gone before my eyes. Some days were more tolerable than others because of Michigan's crazy weather, since there'd been a few warm days in November, of all months, given how far north Lac du Pac Island was. The current temperature, however, complemented my life.

I dug my fists inside the pockets of my jacket while my ears and cheeks felt a slight tingle from the breeze. I walked to Lac du Pac Island State Park and noticed plenty of people over there. Thankfully, no one was on the swings, so I could chill out alone.

I glanced at the swing Kail used to sit on whenever we'd met up in the woods. How was college going for him? Who was his next victim? He'd stolen my heart by pretending to want more with me, and after not getting what he'd *really* been after, *poof*. It'd been over before I'd known it. Well, not before the attempt that had shown his true colors. I didn't miss him at all, and it'd been easier to get over him than I'd thought. Maybe that meant something. Maybe I hadn't really been in love like I'd convinced myself. He'd always be on my mind at some point, though. He was far from a nobody for me to forget about just like that. In fact, I'd carry the bad memories for the rest of my life, and that was what sucked about my experience with him.

My phone chimed with a text notification. I checked it and smiled at the secret lesbian's random opinion about an anime film she'd just watched. I replied, telling her I hadn't seen it yet but that I probably would soon. That excited her, at least, and we got into a brief conversation about it until she announced that her parents needed her for something. Ever since we'd kept in touch through texting, she seemed less depressed. Of course, she could've been withholding stuff for all I knew.

My phone rang, and Ollie's picture appeared on the screen, melting my heart for the millionth time. It was the nice thing about being allowed to be friends out in the open: I could have a picture of him assigned to his contact.

I answered, the giddiness taking control of me. "Hey."

"Jayden, hi! Can you guess where I am?"

I twisted my lips into a curious expression. "Hmm, given your unusual excitement, somewhere outside where your parents can't hear you?"

"I am, yes!" *Someone* was in a good mood. What had gotten into Ollie all of a sudden? But the fact that he was outside gave me hope that we could see each other again. Maybe that was why he was giddy.

"Well, I'm at the state park."

"I'll meet you there!"

"Okay, see you in a few."

"Bye!"

I ended the call and waited on the swing, a dorky smile creeping up on my lips. The things Ollie did to my heart with no effort. I couldn't wait to see him, and after my tiff with Mitch, I could use some good company.

Ugh, Mitch. Why, Mom? Why did she have to meet him? Why did he have to last so long? I wasn't ready for a stepdad, assuming things between them would escalate into something serious. I knew she deserved to be happy after Dad had left us, but I wished she could've chosen a better man. Then again, it wouldn't have mattered if Mitch had been decent because he'd still become a stepdad if he and Mom got serious. I didn't want him in my life, but I felt like he was beginning to be stuck in it against my will. Didn't *I* get a say when it came to Mom's dating life? It affected me too.

"Jayden, hi!"

I snapped back to focus and formed a strong smile at Ollie while he approached me with a similar expression. My heart fluttered like a butterfly at the sight of him, especially his face.

He sat on the swing next to mine on my left side, and sighed in what sounded like a dreamy expression, or maybe he was just relaxed. "So. How are you?"

"I'm good, and you?"

"I feel the same way. My parents let me go out for a walk, so I took advantage and hoped I'd get to see you somewhere outside of school and church."

Ugh, church. I'd already gone twice, and while the

services had been calm and not as crazy as the ones I'd always heard of, they'd been extremely boring. Pastor Belasco definitely knew how to ramble enough about his extreme views, but they'd gone in one ear and out the other. I'd had to fake the occasional smile to avoid any suspicion.

Sadly, after my and Ollie's romantic moment together in the basement of the church, we hadn't repeated that on the second evening this week, and I wondered if Ollie had felt too guilty to do it again. I didn't want to bring it up and risk pressuring him. I'd just have to accept that church really would be all about church and nothing more. We at least sat next to each other, so that helped a tiny bit.

I focused solely on Ollie. "I'm glad you're here. It's great to see you."

"It's great to see *you*. By the way, I submitted my admissions application for Michigan University in Ann Arbor. I did everything early, so I'll probably find out about my acceptance in December."

"Ollie, that's great!"

"It is, yes. I hope I get in."

"I'm sure you will."

"We'll see. If I don't, then it's not a real biggie. There are other schools, but I much prefer this one."

As little as I was interested in this kind of topic, I had to admit I was happy because it meant so much to Ollie. I imagined applying early increased his chances of getting accepted into that university.

Now that we were boyfriends, my future with him crossed my mind more often than not, particularly how things between us would work while he'd be away. While

Ann Arbor wasn't anywhere near as far as Texas was, it was still a distance, and it would mean another important person in my life leaving next fall. I tried so hard to hide my sadness over it, but I failed. I didn't want to be selfish because it was his dream. I just wished it didn't affect our relationship like Sasha's move to Texas would affect my friendship with her.

"Aw, Jayden, what's wrong?"

I gave Ollie a shrug after realizing how silly I was over it. "It's stupid."

"That's not true. Nothing you say is stupid. Tell me what's wrong. Please?"

How could I refuse when it came to Ollie? He made it so easy to talk to him because he accepted me in every single way, and I felt safe confiding in him and relying on our connection. "Well…you're going away next fall. You'll have to live in the dorms. So, I'll probably be stuck here doing nothing but missing you. See? I told you it was stupid."

"Jayden, it's not a real biggie that you feel that way, and it's especially not stupid. It's sweet, actually."

Ollie's words made me feel nice all of a sudden. I liked hearing stuff like that. He could easily spoil me with affection. "Really?"

"I do, yes. Of course. Besides, I'll want to see you every weekend, but we can figure that out later. We still have almost a year before that happens. I'd rather focus on my time here with you. Wouldn't you want to do the same?"

Ollie had a point. I was always the type to worry about the future, so I had to remind myself there was plenty of time to make plans. I looked at him and turned into goo all over again. "Can you say something romantic to me?"

"I can, yes. I think you're beautiful."

Oh? That was *definitely* not what I'd expected. What a compliment! No one had ever called me beautiful before.

"You're the most special person in my life because you're my first love."

The emotions started getting to me in an overwhelming way.

"You woke something in me, and you made me realize just how wonderful it feels to be in love. I feel so lucky to be your boyfriend."

"Oh, Ollie…" I muttered. When I'd told him to speak romance to me, I'd expected something less deep. Deep was better, though. To know he felt all that for me made me realize I'd found the right match. "I feel all those things about you." I did. Ollie was beautiful to me too. He had to be to make me feel the way I did. He had both an outer and inner beauty that made him so perfect.

I felt lucky to be *his* boyfriend.

"Jayden, you know what's even more special?"

"What?"

"We don't have to kiss or have sex to know how we feel about each other."

Have sex. It was the first time I'd heard Ollie say that. I'd never told him about my sexuality, and I wondered how he'd take it. Would he be disappointed knowing he just might never get to experience anything sexual with me? Would it change our relationship forever? I'd never lied to him because he'd never asked, but withholding it felt safer because of my past experience with Kail. While Ollie was definitely no Kail, it didn't guarantee he'd eventually want to take things to the next level. There was a chance he might not want to if he actually believed having sex with a guy was a sin, but I couldn't count on that. No, I wasn't ready to come out to him just yet. I wanted to enjoy what I had with him.

I didn't want to ruin what we had.

My phone chimed with a new text notification, and I grabbed it from my pocket to check the screen. It was from Geoff, which kind of surprised me because we hadn't chatted a whole lot on our own, just the occasional brief exchange of short lines. In his emoji-littered message, he'd asked if I'd like to come over to Sasha's for a game night, and that she was baking chocolate chip cookies to have it with hot cocoa and marshmallows. What a night of fun, and I couldn't wait.

I smiled and replied with my acceptance. It was great that Sasha still thought about me a lot, enough to still want me over despite her busy schedule. After I'd given Geoff a chance, she and I hadn't had any more issues, and Geoff and I continued getting along well. There'd been room for him, after all. With Ollie back in my life, the four of us made a nice circle together.

"Want to go to Sasha's with me for a game night?" I asked. "There's chocolate chip cookies and hot cocoa with marshmallows."

Ollie's eyes lit up with excitement. "I'd like to, yes. That sounds great. Sadly, I can't stay for too long because my parents will eventually expect me back at a reasonable time."

"I get it. We can hang out for a little, play a few board games, and I can walk with you back to your house."

Ollie gave me a big smile. "Jayden, that would be nice. I'd love to walk home with you so that you can keep me company."

I laughed softly. "You act so surprised that I actually want to spend that kind of time with you."

"I'm not surprised, no. I'm just more touched that you always enjoy my company."

"Of course, Ollie. You *literally* make my day every time we're together."

I could tell he melted just like I did because of his dazed expression and lopsided grin. I made him happy, and the fact that he made *me* happy was a plus, because it was mutual. This was something the both of us had never had before. We really did fit perfectly together, and I couldn't stop getting emotional over the reality of finding love.

Ollie sighed. "Jayden, I love you."

Wow, he'd said those words! No guy had ever said them. Well, Kail had been the only one in my life, but Hell would've had to have frozen over for him to tell me that. My heart flittered with bliss. "Aw, I love you, too, Ollie."

He was right. We didn't have to kiss or do anything else intimate for us to feel the way we did. That was what was special about our new relationship. We felt what we felt, and our connection continued to bring us closer.

I really did find love.

Chapter 14

Minutes later, Ollie and I greeted Sasha's parents and went down into the basement. Sasha and Geoff were focused on a game of pool. Geoff played pool really well from what he'd told me, and he and Sasha were serious competitors with how well *she* played.

A mug of root beer with whipped cream and candy sprinkles was set on the bar table, just waiting for Geoff to drink, and it looked freshly made. I wasn't surprised he'd been gaining a little weight from all his favorite American treats. He still looked great, though.

"Hey, guys," I said with a princess wave. "How are you?"

Ollie waved as well, smiling.

"Fine," Geoff said in deep focus, aiming the pool stick at his solid-colored ball. Sasha had the striped-colored ones. He finished his turn and lifted his glasses from sliding. "I try to beat her on this game."

Sasha snorted. "Good luck because I'm already winning."

Geoff smiled as if unaffected. "I have won before, so I

win again this time." He went to take large gulps of his root beer.

She suppressed a laugh. "You only won *one* time, the second game."

Their competitive banter was amusing, and it was nice to see them getting along so well when competing against each other.

"How many games have you played so far?" I asked.

"Oh, God, like…ten, maybe?" Sasha shrugged. "Who knows? I don't remember off the top of my head. It's been a lot, though."

I shook my head, playfully rolling my eyes. "Ugh, pool is *so* boring. I don't get the point of it."

"It's not boring, Jaydles, it's fun. I really wish you'd give it a chance."

"Yah, it's a fun game," Geoff added. He took more gulps and was already almost finished. He let out a little burp and smiled. "Oops, excuse me." I had to admit that he was extra adorable for a moment. Why, I had no idea.

I continued looking at the pool table and questioned what was so special about the game. "I can't see myself having fun playing pool."

"I haven't played pool, actually," Ollie said. "My parents never let me because they see it as a bar game, and they don't like anything to do with bars."

I didn't know what to say to *that*, but his parents needed to go out and touch some grass. We only lived once, after all.

"Sorry to hear that." Sasha frowned.

"Yah," Geoff said with a similar expression. "That's so very sad." He finished his root beer and came closer to us.

"It's not a real biggie," Ollie said as if unaffected. "I do like board games, though, and I've played many of those."

Sasha gasped. "Me too! We should play a board game after this round. I'll have to look through my closet, though. I have *so* many to choose from. What about collectable card games? You like those?"

Ollie suddenly looked geeked out. "I do, yes. I have quite a few of them, actually. Sadly, I don't have anyone to trade with."

"I'll trade with you, and we can play together some time!"

"I'd like that a lot."

"Yay, I'm so animated to find a trading partner."

I sighed. "I think we should stick to board games." Board games were okay, and I'd definitely rather play one of *those* instead of pool or card games.

"Can I come with you?" Ollie asked, beaming. "I'd like to see all the ones you have."

"Of course!" Sasha said. "And we can get a few of them. I can also show you my collectable card games while we're up in my room."

It made my heart tickle just to see how happy Ollie was because he needed that. He needed his time away from his cultlike family and experience life as his true self. It was great he had the ability to do that while at Sasha's.

"I play much board games," Geoff said, "but in German only because English is difficult for me."

"Was it Monopoly?" Ollie asked with extra enthusiasm.

"That was my guess," Sasha added.

"Yah, of course," Geoff said. "Monopoly and the others also. I didn't knew about some from America, but I play anything."

"How about Life?" I asked. "That one's kind of fun."

Sasha beamed even more. "Ooh, I love Life!"

"It's a great game," Ollie said.

I took Ollie's hand and held it, forming a smirk. "We can now use two blue pegs when we get married in the game, since it'll be just us four."

He gave me a dreamy expression, and I was relieved he liked it when I held his hand, especially given that we weren't alone. It was always safe at Sasha's, and it was a great way for us to show affection toward each other. We didn't get that much a whole lot because of school and church, and it was impossible at the park. Well, unless we snuck there late at night, which was a risk.

Sasha gasped. "Aw, look at you two, so adorable! The shipping gods have spoken and answered my humble prayers."

I laughed, and Ollie sheepishly grinned with reddish cheeks.

Even Geoff smiled, totally unfazed because of his support as an ally.

I was actually surprised when Ollie gave my hand a gentle squeeze because it showed he didn't want to stop the affection while probably feeling a bit shy. I could hold his hand all day if given the chance. It was the first time we acted like a couple in front of others, and I was already spoiled by it.

"Oh, we have to get back to the game!" Sasha said. "Unless you guys want to play a board game now?"

"Yah, we must play now the board games," Geoff said.

"I agree," I said. "Let's play a board game now since Ollie can't stay all night." My hand was still in his, and I didn't want to let go of it, but I knew he was too geeked to pass up the chance to see what games Sasha had.

"Okay, but it'll probably be a moment because I still have to bake the cookies."

"Oh, you didn't bake them yet?" I couldn't wait to have a few. Knowing Sasha, they'd be the giant ones with extra chocolate chunks for extra yumminess.

"Nah, I wanted to wait until you and Ollie got here. My mom's making the hot cocoa right now, though, so that should be ready soon. I'll bake the cookies upstairs, too, so I can talk to her for a bit."

"Oh, nice." I loved the way her mom made hot cocoa with some kind of spice, and adding miniature marshmallows was even better.

Sasha beamed. "Come on, Ollie, let's pick out some board games." She led the way and marched up the stairs.

"Jayden, I'll be right back," Ollie said. "Unless you want to come?"

"I'm fine here. I'm curious as to what games you'll choose."

"Is there anything specific you'd like to play?"

"Nope, surprise me."

Ollie smiled and leaned closer to give me a kiss on my cheek. Wow, he'd kissed me! I was definitely surprised about that, and pleasantly so.

I blushed but remained looking into his eyes, and he moved his lips closer to mine for our first kiss. Our lips pressed softly against each other, and while the kiss was little and brief, its meaning was big and everlasting.

I was completely melting.

He gave me one last sheepish grin, then walked away and followed Sasha up the stairs.

I remained standing here with a goofy expression from the kiss—chaste but sweet. It was such a special moment I'd remember for the rest of my life. I was such a total dork, but a dork in love, at least.

"Jayden, you love Ollie, yah?" A warm expression curled Geoff's lips into a smile, telling me how supportive he really was for being a straight guy.

I pretty much mimicked his face except brighter, given the reason. "I do. I've never really felt anything like this. You know, I was involved with someone for a few years, but he didn't feel the same way, and he hurt me."

Geoff's eyebrows flew up. "Oh, no, it's so very sad that he's done those bad things to you."

I shrugged. "Thanks, but luckily I got over it."

"Well, you have now Ollie, so you don't have no more much pains."

"You're right. I don't, at least not like before, anyway. I moved on and found someone worth being with."

"I've got hurt also. She was not good to me, and she's wanted to be with another boy." Geoff briefly frowned but then got back to normal.

"It sucks when that happens, doesn't it?"

"Yah, but it's the life."

I nodded, and the sudden silence felt a little awkward.

"Sasha's told me that you have slept in the guestroom until I've come here. I don't feel good about that because it's your room."

"Oh, don't worry about it. I'll just sleep on the sofa whenever I stay the night again."

It took a moment for Geoff to say another word. "You can sleep on the bed. I'm not bothered."

Aw, he was so adorable to make that offer, but he was the special guest, and it suddenly didn't feel right to have him sleep elsewhere. I had to accept that it was his room until New Year's Eve. I'd been getting over the disappointment over time, anyway. "Thanks, but I couldn't do that. Why would you sleep on the sofa when it's your bed now?"

He flashed a set of well-maintained teeth, clenching in excitement. "No, I don't sleep on the sofa. You sleep with me!"

Oh? I wasn't sure how I felt about *that* offer. It was a little odd because I didn't know him like that, even though he was straight. Maybe sharing a bed was normal to him. Who knew? I let out a tiny laugh. "Geoff, it's *not* that serious. I'll be fine. I mean, would you *really* feel comfortable with that?"

"Why? It's normal with friends. Or friends don't make those things in America?" Wow, he was totally unfazed by this.

"No, we do that. But…I mean…I don't know. We'll see, okay?"

"Yah, okay." Geoff was so friendly and kind, but he also

seemed oblivious to the hidden connotation of the two of us sharing a bed. While we technically were friends, we weren't exactly *friends*, if that made sense. Then again, I did miss the guest bed, and I found myself staring at the guestroom door. I missed sleeping there, but it was his space, and I couldn't invade his privacy like that.

"You miss that room?"

Ugh, had I been obvious? I twisted my lips into a shyish smile. "Meh, it's fine."

He came closer to me, still smiling. "I give you the bed when you stay sometimes here, yah?"

"Geoff, I—"

"No, no, please, Jayden. It's okay. It's not to fear. Sleep on the bed because it's your bed when you stay here. No problems."

Wow, Geoff really *was* a kind person, and generous. He still looked so much like Ollie too. God, it was so unreal that I couldn't stop seeing the resemblance. While they weren't twins or even close to that level of likeness in the face, they shared enough of the same overall features for Geoff to remind me of Ollie almost every time I was around him, like an at-first-glance sort of thing.

I felt a twinge of guilt, but I tried to focus on the fact that Geoff really didn't mind. I sighed in defeat. "Sure, okay, yeah. I'll sleep on your bed."

"Cool! We can be now camp buddies, yah?"

Wait, what? He was *still* planning to sleep on the bed too? I'd totally misunderstood his offer. Sure, he was straight, but it was awkward. I'd also have to tell Ollie about it because I wasn't sure how he'd feel about the situation.

He *clearly* had nothing to worry about, but I didn't want to lie about it either.

"You're a good boy," Geoff said. It was like his overjoyed expression was permanent, not that it bothered me. "I'm so very happy that you want to be my friend."

My heart flittered from his words. To know I was relevant enough to make his day with my being friends with him made me feel good inside. I found myself blushing a little, and I turned away.

He giggled and briefly pointed at my face. "I have made the face so very red. Why?"

I shrugged. "You're just a sweet guy. And honestly? I think you're…kind of special too."

He calmed and just grinned. "You think I'm now special? Like Ollie? Because you've said one time that I and him look like us."

Oh, God, Geoff remembered that! I'd forgotten all about telling him how he'd reminded me of Ollie. Ugh, why was I still blushing like a stupid dork? Maybe the compliment lingered in my head and wouldn't leave me alone. Maybe the compliment mixed with his resemblance to Ollie was the cause of it.

"Okay, so, I say now something," Geoff said. "But don't tell please no one."

I tried to look at him, and the remnants of my unexpected shyness caused me to form just a tiny smile. "I won't tell anyone, no worries. What is it?"

"I'm not gay, but if I would be gay, I'm your type?"

That question? How would I answer it? What did it matter, anyway? He was straight, and Ollie was my boyfriend. It took me a short moment to think of an answer while I formed a pensive face. "If you were gay, and I wasn't with Ollie, then…yeah."

"Because I look like Ollie?"

I let out a soft laugh and blushed all over again. "Maybe? I don't know."

Geoff wrapped his arms around me for a surprising hug, making my heart race. It was a little awkward, given that we weren't *that* close. It was a nice and warm hug, and his light cologne smelled nice, but it was all still awkward, nonetheless. "It feels good to hear that." His voice softened through the hug, and it soothed me in a way I still couldn't explain. "Because if I would be gay, then you're my type also." He let go with an even bigger smile. "For a boy, you're so very beautiful."

I chuckled and struggled to look at him after the hug and especially after *that* compliment. I felt extremely flattered because Ollie had been the only one who'd called me beautiful. Now Geoff, and on the same night! Confusion filled my head, and I didn't know what to think. I'd known straight guys my whole life, and they'd *never* said those things about other guys. Maybe he really *was* that liberal. He was from Berlin, after all.

"Jayden?"

"Yeah?"

"If I would be gay…then I kiss you if you would want that."

The sounds of footsteps clomping down startled me, and Geoff wasted no time moving away to give ourselves some distance. As soon as Sasha and Ollie appeared, I felt relieved, and I couldn't explain why. She carried a large tray of giant chocolate chip cookies while Ollie carried a stack of board games. They set them down on the bar table near me.

"I'll be back again," Sasha said. "I'm getting the mugs of hot cocoa and a bag of marshmallows." She marched back upstairs.

Ollie's wide smile melted my heart, and I suddenly needed his affection after an awkward moment with Geoff. I knew Geoff had meant well, but he needed to learn a few things about socializing, particularly the hidden rules that most people naturally knew to follow.

I gave Ollie a hug and buried my face in his shoulder, inhaling his natural scent with a hint of soap.

"Aw, Jayden, did you miss me?"

"I did." I remembered that Geoff was still here, and I decided to cut the hug short to prevent *him* from possibly feeling awkward. I glanced at him and noticed a weaker expression, and I felt a little bad. Maybe the affection made him more uncomfortable than I'd thought. Maybe it had triggered what he used to have with his ex-girlfriend.

Ollie was so geeked out again that he rushed to the table and perused the boxes of board games, probably deciding which to play. He was absorbed by his enthusiasm, and it was adorable. I couldn't keep my eyes off him, and my heart couldn't stop feeling strong things for him.

I cast my eyes on Geoff who'd already been looking at me, but something seemed to have bothered him. I couldn't put my finger on it, but I hoped he was okay. The last thing I needed was to make him feel uncomfortable after we'd become friends.

He grabbed his phone and began typing something.

My phone immediately chimed with a message notification after he finished. That must've been for me since the chime was from the chat app we used. I grabbed my phone and checked the message.

Geoff: *I hope, that you are happy with Ollie! :)*

But when I looked back at him, his face didn't match the smiley one he'd messaged me. The corners of his mouth were a little lowered, and he looked away. What was bothering him? Had I triggered something?

I replied to his message by asking if he was okay.

Geoff: *You and Ollie together remember me when I have had someone special in my life and I miss that. :(*

Aw, poor Geoff. So, that was what it was. My heart cracked for him because he probably missed his old girlfriend. I wondered if there was a girl on the island who'd like him, but I couldn't think of who, and I totally didn't have it in me to play matchmaker for him. Oh, well. I knew exactly what I had to do and what I wanted to do. I'd focus on being a closer friend to him in hopes that we'd grow closer and bond the way Sasha and I bonded.

I'd spend more time with Geoff from now on.

Chapter 15

On Sunday, we sat through two hours of Bible study. Despite being bored out of my mind, I'd at least gotten to sit next to Ollie again, and no one had been suspicious the entire time. Well, I questioned whether Gracie was an exception because she was suddenly hard to read. Either she did suspect I was up to something, or she was too stunned by my church presence to say a word to me.

Ollie and I got up from our pew, and Pastor Belasco smiled at us. "Jayden, can I speak to you in my office for a moment?"

Ollie gave me a happy expression. "I'll wait for you here, okay?"

I nodded and followed Pastor Belasco into his office, which was the left of the two doors on either side of the altar. I took a seat and observed the tiny room. There was just a small desk and chair, and two chairs in front of the desk. The walls had a couple of inspirational posters for all ages, mostly family-themed.

Pastor Belasco closed the door, then cleared some of the clutter on the surface of his desk and sat down.

I glanced at a picture frame facing me. It was of Ollie, his older brother and sister, and their parents, all of them with what looked like forced smiles. They resembled a lot of each other. Pastor Belasco shared the most features with Ollie, like a forty-something version of him with minor differences.

Pastor Belasco formed a tight smile. "This is your third time coming to church, and I'm honestly impressed."

I smiled, feeling relieved that my plan had been working. I wasn't sure what I'd do without Ollie in my life, but I'd had a painful preview of it not too long ago. I could only imagine it'd be worse now that I was in love with him. "Thanks."

He sighed, looking more serious. "But it's bull, and we both know it."

My jaw almost dropped, and my heart stopped for a moment. "Wh-what do you mean?"

He didn't seem angry, but he looked very uncomfortable now, which intensified my anxiety. "Gracie overheard a private conversation between you and Ollie in the basement."

Oh. My. God. Had that fourteen-year-old brat seriously been eavesdropping the whole time? I hadn't heard anyone at all. Ugh, she must've been as quiet as a cat with her footsteps, probably listening from halfway down the stairs.

"She told me things that bothered me. And frankly, I'm hurt that you lied to me and my wife about your interest in being saved."

I inhaled and exhaled, frowning. I was caught with no

way out of the lie. Just when I'd found a way to be with Ollie, Gracie had had to yank it away for the second time.

"Why, Jayden? Why would you lie like that?"

It took me a while to say something, trying my hardest to calm down. "I wanted to spend time with Ollie."

"You mean, you wanted to see if you can get him to be your boyfriend, which you succeeded in doing, according to Gracie."

Yep, Pastor Belasco knew everything, and there was no escaping the truth.

"Well, I don't accept that, Jayden. My son is *not* gay, and all you're doing is confusing him."

I swallowed a lump in my throat, finding it challenging to argue with someone so deep in denial because of his homophobic views. My eyes watered, and my body trembled. Was it over again between me and Ollie? "Pastor Belasco...I love Ollie with all my heart. And that's not a lie."

He let out a deep breath and rubbed his temples. "Jayden, homosexuality is a sin. God does send sinners like you to Hell. You're now putting my son in danger with your terrible influence. He's losing his morals because of you, and I can't allow that to continue."

My first tear rolled down my cheek. "Why are you so full of hate?" My voice was too weak to argue. The defeat weighed me down.

"Oh, Jayden, I don't hate you. I hate your sin, but not *you*."

"If it's any consolation, I haven't had sex with anyone, so if homosexuality really is a sin, then how can I go to Hell for loving Ollie if we're never going to have sex?" Of course, I didn't hold any Christian views, but it was worth a try.

"Because it's still ungodly. God created relationships to be between one man and one woman. Any other kind of relationship is not righteous or pure in God's eyes. And I'm sorry, but the kind of love you claim you feel for Ollie isn't possible. That exists only between a man and a woman. Or in your case, a boy and a girl. You're confused, Jayden, plain and simple."

I couldn't believe the toxic words that had just come out of Pastor Belasco's mouth. He was so against same-sex relationships that even the sexless ones offended him. "I'm not confused. I know what I feel."

"No, you *think* you know what you feel. Don't you see, Jayden? The Devil is luring you into his world of sin. It may feel like real love, but that's only because it's the Devil filling your head with lies. That's the point, so that you can sin against God."

While I'd already known what Pastor Belasco's views were, having an actual private discussion about it heightened my realization of it. My blood started boiling at the thought of Gracie, and my hatred for her intensified.

"Listen, Jayden, I don't want to see you destroy your life over sin. I want to see you do right in God's eyes. I'd like you to keep coming to church. Now, I will say this. You can no longer be around Ollie, but you're still more than welcome to keep attending because *all* lost souls are welcome in the house of the Lord."

"You act like I'm a disease."

"I didn't say you were, but your confusion is turning you

into a bad influence on Ollie. He's my *son*, Jayden. My little *boy*. I can't let you be near him. I'm sorry, but I can't. I love him too much to let you cause him any harm."

The depression of losing Ollie hit me so hard that the urge to cry came at me in large waves, threatening to lose my control. My lips quivered, and more tears rolled down my face.

"I really do care about you, or else I wouldn't be saying any of this. You're not a bad person by nature, you're just misguided, and that's what the Devil wants. He wants to steer you toward the wrong path, but you still have a chance to be saved. It's not too late."

Then, that was it. I burst into heavy sobs.

"Oh, Jayden, please don't cry," Pastor Belasco said in a soft tone. Was he hurt too? His face looked pained, but he was still a toxic person whose words I'd never accept as true.

I couldn't stop bawling, but I tried to be silent in case Ollie could hear from how small the church was.

Pastor Belasco sighed. "Can I trust you with a secret that no one knows? Not Ollie, not even my wife."

That suddenly piqued my curiosity, but I was still an emotional mess. I just gave him a weak nod.

"First, I need you to promise me that you'll keep this between us." Pastor Belasco's face showed that he was deeply worried, maybe scared.

I didn't want to hurt anyone, not even Gracie. I just wanted Ollie back. At the same time, I wanted to know just what Pastor Belasco was hiding. I sniffled a few times. "I promise," I mumbled.

It took him a moment, and he swallowed. He let out a

stuttered breath as if stalling a bit, and his eyes were misty. "I was confused at one point in my life, just like you."

I finally stopped crying and wiped my face, sniffling again. I lowered my eyebrows, unsure if what he was trying to say was what I suddenly suspected. "Confused?"

"Yes. Without getting too much into it, let's just say I personally know what you're going through."

Oh. My. God. Pastor Belasco was gay? I couldn't believe my ears, and shock was an understatement. "Oh…"

"But that's all in the past now. I'm healed, and you can be too."

I remembered when Ollie had researched about the different groups of gay Christians when it came to views on homosexuality: Side A who believed it wasn't a sin, and Side B who believed it was. He'd then told me about Side X who believed in conversion through various methods. Of course, he'd had no idea that his own dad had turned out to be one of them.

"Pastor Belasco," I said in a slightly stronger voice. "That's impossible."

"I understand why you'd believe that, but it's actually not. I thought the same way, too, trust me. But you know, you still have a chance because…you haven't had sex yet, right?"

I shook my head, finding the question to be extremely uncomfortable.

"Well, I have. Many times. So, that should tell you that if *I* can be healed, so can you."

For the first time, I actually felt sorry for Pastor

Belasco. He wasn't a bad person. He'd never been. He was just in denial, confused. He probably hated himself for it.

"It's why I worry so much about Ollie. I don't believe he's gay like I used to be. I believe he's just confused."

I gave Pastor Belasco a headshake, wishing I could help him see the truth. "You're wrong. You just don't want to accept it."

"No, Jayden. *You* are confused, not me."

"Maybe you blame yourself because you feel like you failed Ollie?"

Pastor Belasco paused, his eyes focusing deeply on me. He pursed his lips and inhaled through his nostrils, his cheeks reddening. "That's not an appropriate thing to say. You crossed the line with that question." Was he mad? Had I struck a nerve?

"I didn't mean to offend you."

"Well, you did. You're basically saying that I was a failure for not raising my son right, and that's just not true."

"I'm sorry, Pastor Belasco. I wasn't trying to disrespect you or anything. I just thought maybe the reason why you don't accept that Ollie is gay is because *you're* gay, and you feel like you had something to do with it when you really didn't."

Pastor Belasco sighed. "I think we're done here."

"Oh…" I lowered my gaze and frowned. What more could I say? Nothing seemed to work. His repression was so deep that he'd convinced himself he was no longer gay, and as painful as it was to hear that, as much as I wished I could help him, it was beyond my control. I only hoped he could accept himself one day in the future.

"Like I said before, you're still welcome here, but you can't sit with Ollie anymore, and you can no longer talk to or hang out with him. It's over, Jayden. I'm breaking you two up. And don't worry about telling him because he and I will have a private talk later at home."

There was my depression again, the reality forming another storm cloud to last for a while. Why, Gracie? Had she never butted in, Ollie and I would've still been together. We were suddenly forced to break up, and it pained me so much to accept it.

It killed me.

Pastor Belasco softened his expression. "You take care, Jayden. May God actually be with you this time."

I didn't bother with a reply. I got up, opened the door, and Ollie was still here, the only one left. He'd been waiting for me the whole time, and that big smile of his that told me how much he'd probably missed me for the moment I'd been away suddenly threatened me to emotionally burst all over again. I wasn't allowed to talk to him anymore, and I was afraid to get him into more trouble. With tears on my face, I rushed past him and stormed out, the fresh air much less suffocating than the atmosphere inside the church.

"Jayden, wait!"

I stopped and turned around with a few sniffles. I waited for Ollie to reach me, and I needed his arms around me. I didn't care who was around, just random residents and maybe a few church members.

"What happened? Did my dad say something to make you cry?"

I sniffled some more and wiped my tears, nodding. "It's over," I muttered.

Ollie sighed with a frown. "Jayden...please don't say that."

"It's true. I don't want it to be over, but we have no choice. Gracie heard us in the basement the one time, and she told your dad everything. He forced me to end it with you."

"Oh, great. Not again."

Ugh, it was like déjà vu. "No one ever wants to leave us alone. They keep breaking us apart."

"I've never stopped fighting for you, and I never will." Ollie started breathing in and out. Since his eyes were misty, I wasn't sure if he was nervous, sad, upset, or what. "I can't believe I'm going to do this, but..." He wrapped his arms around me and gave me the deepest kiss he'd ever given me, both shocking my mind and melting my heart. The tips of our tongues touched several times, and our lips massaged each other in a lengthy, soft kiss. I ignored the footsteps approaching us, but not for long.

Ollie was yanked away from me, and Pastor Belasco gave me a threatening stare while gripping Ollie's arm. "That's enough, Jayden! If you don't leave my son alone, I'll have the authorities involved and put a restraining order on you."

I wasn't nervous around Pastor Belasco anymore, given what he'd confessed to me in private, and the defiance flowed through my veins. "You might be able to stop us from seeing each other, but you'll never stop us from loving each other." I gave Ollie a final glimpse, my heart sinking all the way into the depths of depression. "I love you."

His eyes watered. "I love you, too," he said under his breath.

Our eyes locked with one another, and we cried softly, but it didn't last long. Pastor Belasco grabbed him by the arm in anger and whisked him away by force. That was it. That was the end of us.

And I suddenly felt dead inside.

Chapter 16

On Wednesday, I was alone at my locker; there were just a few other students in the hallway. I hadn't talked a whole lot since the forced breakup. I also hadn't bothered with going to church since the plan had foiled. I'd barely seen Ollie, just a few glimpses at school, but I knew he was as hurt and depressed as I was.

I'd called Sasha immediately when I'd gotten home on Sunday. I'd cried over the phone, staying in my room for most of the day. She'd been such a great friend and had tried to make me feel better, even trying to get me to come over, but I couldn't. I was *so* depressed that it paralyzed me with a loss of motivation. I'd even made room to complain about Mitch, but because she didn't know him, she never said much about him.

I'd also vented to the secret lesbian without going too much into detail, since we still weren't close. She'd at least expressed sympathy, but unfortunately, she didn't have much else to say.

A hand softly gripped my shoulder, and Geoff stood to

my right with a genuinely concerned expression. "How you are, Jayden?"

I could hardly look at him without feeling emotional. I stared at the inside of my locker until my eyes watered for the millionth time. "I miss him, Geoff." My voice was too weak for me to carry on a conversation.

"I know. I'm sad about those bad things about you."

I breathed in, held my breath, and let it all out. My heart felt heavy, and I wished the pain could go away so that I could move on. That was the thing, though. I wasn't sure if I'd ever move on from Ollie. I'd fallen harder for him than I'd thought, and losing him forever made me realize it more. A tear rolled down my cheeks, and I knew I'd end up crying all over again.

"Aw, Jayden, please, don't cry."

But I did. Hard.

Geoff surprised me by wrapping his arms around me, making my heart race, and it suddenly felt so right to have this kind of affection and support. His light cologne smelled so amazingly nice, though, even better than Kail's stronger and sportier one, and I could get used to it fast. That, his overall looks, and his deepish and soothing voice made for a nice package. But the hug was more important, and I wanted to focus on our friendship and his support.

I would've wanted a hug from Sasha, too, but she wasn't around right now. She was in pre-calc, the only class we didn't have together.

At least Geoff had been so sweet the entire time, and while we hadn't done voice or video chat on the app we used, we still texted, even though it wasn't a whole lot. He'd given me a bunch of heart and hug emojis in his messages too.

I'd needed this hug, though. It was longer than the first one he'd given me, and it felt warmer and comfier. He and Sasha had tried to console me at school the past two days, but it'd been useless. This hug wasn't useless, though. While I couldn't heal from it, I didn't want to let go of Geoff.

"Hmm, two dudes hugging," said a random boy in a loud voice as he walked past us. "Okay, then."

Geoff was quick to let me go, and he eyed the boy with what looked like contempt. "He's my good friend and he has much pains also!"

The boy just shook his head as if in disbelief while continuing ahead.

As if *that* hadn't been enough, Gracie magically appeared walking toward me with the smuggest expression I'd ever seen on her. She leaned against the locker to the left of mine, opposite of Geoff, hugging a large Bible as if clinging onto the angelic morality she believed she upheld. She looked more comfortable and less socially reserved than before. She'd won, after all. "I see you move on quickly."

I scoffed and gave her a grimace. "What are you talking about? I haven't moved on from Ollie at all."

"That's not what it looked like to me just now."

Oh. The hug. God, she really had a lot of nerve to come up to me and start drama while flaunting her triumph. What more could she ask for when she'd already gotten what she'd wanted?

"I'm not surprised, though," she continued. "He *does* look a little like Ollie at first glance, so it makes sense."

Geoff definitely didn't like her from the expression he made, his eyes glued to her appearance. "You're not right because I'm not gay. And you're not a nice person also because you make those bad things to Jayden."

Gracie didn't seem mad, though. The subtle smirk just itching to form on her lips said it all. "Maybe you need to learn more English before you have room to criticize me."

Geoff immediately shut up, his face red with anger. I wasn't sure if he felt offended, since he had his struggles with English.

Ugh, I'd had enough of this drama. I couldn't take it anymore. The scheming, the winning, and the flaunting, all rolled into one mean-girl package. Who did she think she was? I slammed my locker shut and then slammed my hand hard against the locker door, startling Gracie enough to drop her Bible on the floor. I didn't care if the few students around us stopped everything to witness the scene I'd just caused.

From her expression, she was either stunned, scared, or both. Good.

Geoff frowned. "Jayden, don't fight, please?"

A boy and a girl stopped near us as if to butt in. The boy looked at the Bible on the floor and then at Gracie, lowering his eyebrows with suspicion. "Did he just push you against the locker?"

Gracie quickly grabbed her Bible and hugged it to her chest, lowering her head with a frown that didn't match the triumph she'd felt before. She formed a pout as her response, remaining silent.

I gave the boy and girl a set of pleading eyes, my heart

racing because the last thing I'd want was for anyone to think I was capable of physical violence. Even a few other students stared at us. "I didn't push her, I swear!"

"He don't never do that," Geoff added for me, always having my back when I needed him.

Gracie still didn't say a word, her convincing victimization serving as her weapon. What a scared face that deserved an award.

The boy and girl shook their heads and walked away, along with a few other students abandoning the scene. Who knew if they believed a word I'd said, or the silence Gracie had retained.

I suddenly couldn't control my anger or the intense hatred I'd felt toward her for a long time, and I faced her with a contemptuous gaze. "Congrats, Gracie. You hurt me just like you planned."

"H-how did I hurt you?" Her eyes glistened, and the smugness from her triumph immediately vanished.

"You overheard me and Ollie during a private conversation, and you just *had* to tell his dad everything. Of course, because you knew he'd break us up so you can have Ollie all to yourself."

Gracie kept quiet.

"You have *no* heart, because if you *did*, you wouldn't have destroyed what me and Ollie had, and that sent me into a deep depression these past few days. But of course, you don't care about that. You only care about what *you* want. And the fact that you call yourself a Christian while plotting mean drama against me is disgusting. You're a mean, vile person, and I wish you never existed on this planet."

Gracie's eyes watered, her lips quivered, and she looked like she was about to cry. Speechless, she hugged her Bible more tightly and walked away in a rushed pace, her skirt flapping around her ankles while her French-braided pigtails bounced on her back. An innocent look on a not-so-innocent girl.

I let out a deep breath, confusion filling my head. My anger morphed into sadness. I couldn't believe I'd confronted a fourteen-year-old girl like that, making her cry. Had I been too mean with my words? I'd been so angry with hatred over her that I couldn't have controlled myself. What she'd done was mean too. I couldn't get over the fact that she'd sabotaged what I'd had with Ollie, and willingly.

Geoff came closer to me and managed a weak smile, but he didn't say a word.

"Was I harsh?" I asked. Why was I worried all of a sudden?

"Yah, but you must not fear her like that also. That was not nice, Jayden."

He had a point, and I started regretting the confrontation because it had probably hurt her more than I'd thought. I was torn between remorse and revenge. "Yeah, you're right. Sorry about that."

"No, you say sorry to her, not to me. But she was not nice with those bad things to you also. You must say sorry to each other and make two peaces for both."

My mouth corners drooped, and the depression killed my mood once more. "I just want the pain to stop."

Geoff grabbed my arm with a gentle grip, his frown deepening. "I know, Jayden. I don't want you to have those pains. I'm sad also."

I had to admit that it was good having him in my life. While it wasn't exactly a cure for my depression, it was better than being completely alone. I had him and Sasha, and they were such great friends. What would I do without them?

The clacking of heels prompted me to turn around, and Principal Olsen marched up to me and cleared her throat.

I captured her stern-looking face, and after seeing Gracie standing behind her in tears, I knew I was in deep trouble for what I'd said. I swallowed a lump in my throat.

"Jayden, I need you to come to my office. *Now*."

"Am…I in trouble?"

"Oh, believe me. You certainly are after what Gracie just reported to me."

I wasn't sure what kind of trouble I'd be in, but as I glanced at Gracie, she was far from subtle with forming a triumphant smirk that told me all it needed to tell me.

She wasn't hurt one bit.

Chapter 17

A few minutes later, I was in Principal Olsen's office across from her desk, sitting on the chair to Gracie's left with ample distance between us. I lowered my head and hoped whatever punishment I received wouldn't be too harsh. Of course, by now, Gracie's smirk had already vanished, replaced by her angelic mask. And she *still* hugged her Bible.

Principal Olsen sighed, her eyes exuding a controlled kind of anger that continued to intimidate me. "Gracie told me you pushed her against the lockers, and there are several other witnesses who can confirm that."

What...? It took me a while to respond, but there was no point in pleading my case. How could I convince them otherwise when the "witnesses" to the "push" clearly saw what they wanted to see? I had no choice but to serve whatever punishment I needed to be slapped with. I should've never confronted Grace to begin with, but it'd been impossible not to cause a scene, given the circumstances. "I did cause a scene." My voice was weak, and I felt defeated. However, Hell would freeze over for me to actually say I pushed her.

"And that you said some really nasty things to her that made her cry."

Given the truth about that part, it probably made the push and false witnesses believable. "I was just mad."

"Jayden, regardless of how angry you are, you do *not* encourage suicide to anyone."

I jolted upright in my seat. "Wait, what? I didn't do that!"

"You didn't tell her that you wished she didn't exist on this planet?"

Oh. That. Wow, I hadn't meant suicide at all! Way to twist my words in a whole different direction. "It wasn't like that, though. I just...I..." I didn't even know how to explain myself. What could I say? I'd said it, and I could suddenly see why it could easily be misconstrued.

"You're going on eighteen, *almost* an adult, and she's only fourteen," Principal Olsen said with focused eyes on the two of us. "You should know better than that. Please apologize to her."

I turned my head and struggled to focus on Gracie, given my disdain. I had to, though. At the end of the day, I'd been mean, too, no matter how angry I'd been. Even Geoff had wanted us to apologize to each other. "I'm sorry for causing a scene. And for all the things I said. I didn't mean it as suicide, but I guess I can see how you'd think that."

Gracie didn't say a word, but her "hurt" face definitely didn't fool me. If only my fate here wasn't on the line.

"I was…furious. Because you took Ollie away from me. You told his dad about us knowing he'd force us to break up." The painful memory hit me hard, and I didn't care if I was on the verge of tears. "I want to know why you did it. And why do you hate me so much?"

Gracie let out a deep breath, but I still didn't buy her expression. She was most likely faking every single thing in Principal Olsen's office. "I never said I hated you."

"Yeah, well, you do. Back when I was in the ninth grade, when I met you as part of the DORK bond, you were kind of unfriendly to me. Why?"

After moments of being quiet, Gracie finally spoke. "You're not the only who loves Ollie."

I'd known that already, but it was surprising she'd actually confessed it. It was about time, and I suddenly wanted a serious conversation about it with her because it was time to put our social war to bed. I was sick of it. I wanted her to leave me alone for good, but I also wanted to stop being a target of hate.

I sighed, realizing that Principal Olsen was still focused on us and probably expecting us to resolve our issues. "He's gay, though."

Gracie shook her head. "No, he's confused."

Oh. My. God. Not *this* again! "It's really sad how you can't accept people for being different. He's just going to end up resenting you someday, if he hasn't already, and when he turns eighteen soon and goes away to college next fall, you'll never see him again, anyway. So, why bother? He's gay, Gracie. Get that through your head."

"He's *not* gay. *Stop* saying that. *You* were the one who

took him away from me. When you first joined the DORK bond, he was already starting to pay less attention to me when we used to be closer. *You* stole him from me, *not* the other way around like you keep saying."

I didn't know what to say to that specifically. It wasn't like I'd meant to do it, but she'd never believe a word I said. She was too far gone with her delusions, and she couldn't even accept that Ollie was gay simply because she constantly prayed she'd have a chance with him.

"Any homosexual stuff that went on after that was because of you. You *made* him that way with your bad influence."

Principal Olsen cleared her throat and gave Gracie a tight and tiny smile. "Despite the island being more on the conservative side, we do not tolerate bigotry at this school. So, please watch your language."

Gracie shut up instantly, and I tried to mask whatever smug feeling *I* now felt. Most of all, I was surprised Principal Olsen was tolerant of my sexuality. Whether she personally supported the LGBTQ community was yet to be known, and I wouldn't ask her that. However, she was against discrimination, and that was what mattered to me.

"Gracie, I understand you have your views," Principal Olsen continued, "and that you're very passionate about them, but to accuse someone of turning them gay? I'd like to believe you know better than that."

"I'm a Christian. It goes against God, and I'm against everything that God's against."

"That doesn't change our school policy on discrimination."

I had to admit that the more Principal Olsen talked, the safer I felt. She really was on my side, after all. It touched my heart to get to know that side of her.

Gracie looked at me as if with contempt, or so her eyes hinted to me. "You're not going to Heaven no matter how hard you try to change."

"Gracie, that's *enough*," Principal Olsen said in almost a bark, her eyes full of warning.

After a brief pause, Gracie sighed. "Can I please go now, Principal Olsen?"

Principal Olsen calmed. "Yes, you may leave."

Gracie got up while still hugging her Bible, and she rudely brushed past me toward the door like I'd been in her way. She stopped for a moment while Principal Olsen wasn't looking, and she gave me the most evil expression I'd ever seen on her face. Finally, she left.

I looked down and drew a big breath. I wanted to believe she'd leave me alone from now on. After all, what more drama could she cause? She'd already won Ollie as her prize, even though he'd never have feelings for her. "Thanks, Principal Olsen. Have a nice day." I got up from my seat.

"Uh-uh, sit down." Her stern tone returned.

I dropped right back on my seat and stifled a groan. What now?

Principal Olsen eyed me like a hawk. "Jayden, I may not tolerate any kind of bigotry because of my support for the LGBTQ community, but that doesn't excuse you from pushing Gracie against the lockers and insinuating suicide."

Of course. Principal Olsen wasn't going to let it go. "I

understand. But can I at least admit something to you?" I hoped my words could be convincing enough.

"Go ahead."

"I actually didn't push Gracie. I slammed my hand against the locker and it caused her to drop her Bible. I guess whoever the witnesses are must've thought I pushed her."

Principal Olsen sighed. "Jayden, while you do look like you're telling the truth, and I'd like to believe you didn't push Gracie, unfortunately, it's your word against hers, so we have to manage this without taking sides. There are witnesses, after all, and I cannot argue against that, especially given the things you said to her."

The defeat weighed me down, and I realized it was futile to keep pleading my case.

"As a result, I'm suspending you for one week, starting today."

My eyes bulged, and my mouth dropped open. "What?"

"Jayden, you could've physically hurt her, and given how young and impressionable she is, who's to say she wouldn't have felt suicidal over what you said to her? The fact that you're almost an adult *male* warring against a teenage *girl* in this manner doesn't sit well with our society, religious or not. That can be seen as harassment."

Principal Olsen did have a point. I'd never looked at it that way, and I felt worse. I might've hated Gracie, but I didn't actually want her dead. "I don't wish death on her."

"That's not the point, Jayden. What happens if the school did nothing about the situation and she tells her parents about it? They could take legal action."

"I didn't realize that, Principal Olsen," I muttered.

"Well, hopefully now you do. On top of the suspension, I expect a two-page essay on why you did what you did, and what you plan to do to change your behavior, including an apology somewhere in the text."

I slipped out a whiny groan. "Really?"

"Yes, really? Do you think I'm joking about any of this?"

I shook my head, and my entire day had officially been ruined. I'd never been suspended in my life. Then again, I'd never pushed anyone or tried to fight with someone. I deserved it for the things I'd said, though, and it made me regret being so angry. As much as I hated Gracie, I had to move on. At least she was finally out of my life.

For good.

Chapter 18

It was late afternoon on Saturday. I hadn't gone out last night, even though Sasha had invited me over, so today suddenly made me want to change that. I was in my room, and I didn't want to mope around anymore. Tomorrow would be one week since my and Ollie's forced breakup, and I was still suspended from school with a boring essay to prepare for. I wanted to take my mind off things.

My phone chimed with a text notification, and I checked the screen. It was a message from the secret lesbian.

T.S.L.: *Why did I have to be born this way when the world already didn't accept me? Why can't I like guys instead? Life would be so much easier.*

She was going through her internalized homophobia again after being fine for a while, but I'd forgotten how difficult it was for her. I told her to hang in there and that we could chat if he was up for it. She was, and we chatted for quite a while until she had to go. I hoped she'd get better.

I grabbed my clean clothes and towel to get ready for a shower, and I walked into the living room and rolled my eyes at Mitch who was on the long couch. Mom sat next to him, and I realized more that things between them really *had* been working out.

And I didn't like it one bit.

Mom and Mitch cackled at the TV while beer cans littered the coffee table. Some stand-up comedy show was on, and I couldn't care less about the biker-looking comedian and his unfunny jokes.

I shook my head and needed to get away.

"Hey, Jayden!" Mitch waved at me with a drunk smile while Mom lit up a cigarette. "Your mom told me about the suspension. Good on you for sticking up for your beliefs."

I looked at him and tried not to snap from being annoyed by him. "Yeah, well, she was a religious bigot who managed to destroy my relationship with the *one* guy I loved because *she* wants him."

Mom puffed some smoke and let out a raspy chuckle. "What a delusional twit. You'll find a better boyfriend, Jayden. Maybe someone *not* religious this time."

"I'm not in a rush for someone new."

"Nothing wrong with that. I never even got to meet Ollie personally. Was he at least good to you?"

I was surprised Mom wanted to make conversation all of a sudden. That was weird. "He was. He was sweet, kind, affectionate, and he loved me. But his dad made us break up, so we can't see each other ever again."

"Sorry to hear that, Jayden," Mitch said with a weaker smile despite being drunk. I didn't care about what he had to say. He'd already overstayed his welcome, and it was time he'd finally be hauled away in a truck for good.

If only.

"Anyway, I'm going to take a shower," I said in an apathetic tone. "I'm going out to Sasha's." I rushed into the bathroom for a long shower until the water got cold, probably about a half hour. After I got out and headed back into the living room, Mom and Mitch were gone.

I heard Mom's raspy laugh from her bedroom with the door closed, and I figured they were hanging out.

"Come on, Marsha," Mitch said in a weird voice that was probably supposed to be sexy—whatever "sexy" meant. "Stop teasing the big beast and put it in already."

Oh. My. God. My ears, my ears…

Grimacing, I rushed inside my room to grab my thick jacket because of the temperature outside. While I had no idea where I'd go, I was desperate to leave the house to avoid being stuck listening to them. It was either that or having to listen to music with my earbuds nonstop for what could be hours.

I left the house in no time, grabbing my phone to call Sasha. She'd invited me over many times since the forced breakup, only for me to decline each time, but not anymore. I needed to snap out of this funk. I wished the temperature hadn't been getting colder as the days passed by because there was no comfortable way to hang out at any of the parks or even go on a carriage ride. Sasha's house was pretty much the only place to go.

She answered my call almost immediately. "Please tell me you're finally coming over or I'll scream."

"Oh, believe me, Sash, I am."

"Yay, I'm so animated!"

"I don't want to be depressed anymore. At least not for tonight. It sucks, and I hate feeling this way. I also hate that I'm suspended while having to write a stupid essay that won't mean anything." Well, technically, I did feel remorse over accidentally implying suicide, but I didn't need to write two full pages to express that.

"Have you started on it yet?"

"No, probably in the week, but I have to have it done by Thursday when I come back to school. Ugh, it's like first I lose Ollie, now this. And Gracie gets away with everything as usual."

"I've officially lost all respect for her as a person, and to think I used to get along with her back when we were in the DORK bond. I mean, yeah, I admit saying what you said to her wasn't a good idea, but I don't think she'll ever like you."

"I don't either. I guess we were meant to be enemies. I wish I could stop thinking about it. That and Ollie. And I *still* can't stand Mitch. I'll never understand what Mom sees in him."

"Well, like I've said before, you didn't use to like Geoff at one point, so maybe it'll eventually be that way with Mitch?"

"I doubt that. Ugh, I wish I could be fine and not have to deal with any more drama."

"Don't worry, Jaydles, we'll find plenty to do to get you distracted. Want to bake something again?"

I could use some tasty treats, and a glass of milk would go along great with cookies. "How about we go crazy with sweets and make Great Eight cookies?"

"Ooh, I haven't made Great Eight cookies in forever. You still want the same eight ingredients, right?"

"Of course, that's the point. What were they again? I always forget one of them."

"Milk chocolate chips, white chocolate chips, M&M's, Reese's Pieces, peanut butter, oatmeal, raisins, and crushed nuts."

"You got it!" As depressed as I still was, my mood did lift a tiny bit at the thought of hybrid cookies.

"Awesome, and it'll be Geoff's first time trying them."

"He might like them, right?"

"He loves anything sweet, so I'm sure."

"That's good. Well, I'll see you in a few."

"Okay, bye!"

I ended the call and managed a little smile with some weakness trying to flip it back upside down. I wished I could barge into Holy Light of Emmanuel, offer Ollie the chance to run away with me, take the ferry together, and never come back. Of course, if he agreed to it, I'd have no idea where we'd go from there.

Then again, anywhere was better than here.

Chapter 19

Minutes later, I arrived and greeted Sasha's parents, and I went down into the basement where she was baking the cookies. That was fast. I glanced at the bar table and wasn't surprised to see a half-finished mug of what was most likely root beer with melted whipped cream and a few candy sprinkles left. I bet Geoff would probably never get tired of drinking that while he was here in the U.S.

I managed a princess wave, a weak smile spanning my lips. "Hey."

"Hey, Jaydles! I *just* put the cookies in the oven. My mom's using the one in the upstairs kitchen, that's why."

"Wow, you haven't used the basement one in *so* long."

"Nope, since there's usually no need to. At least it's convenient since we're going to be hanging out here, anyway."

"True." I suddenly heard Geoff's muffled voice from a distance behind the closed guestroom door, and he was speaking German. "Is he busy?"

"He's doing video chat with his family. He should be done soon since it's almost midnight in Germany."

"Oh, right. They're six hours ahead of us."

"Yep. He just had *two* root beer floats on top of the drink you see there."

My eyebrows flew up. "Wow, he's going to gain more weight if he doesn't tone it down."

"He does look a little *thicc* nowadays, I admit, but he doesn't seem to care, and that's perfectly fine by me. I'm more worried that he'll get sick at some point because he devours all that sugary junk almost every day, and he uses the bathroom a lot because of it."

"Is he lactose-intolerant?"

"I've actually wondered that. I did hear him in the bathroom a few times groaning like he was in pain. I mean, we're all fat here and so are my sisters, but we don't eat junk food to *that* extent."

"Have you thought about telling him to take it easy?"

"Eh. You know us, especially my parents. We treat him like our own here, and whatever he wants to eat or drink, we get it for him because it's really no problem for us, and he's never demanding about it, so that helps."

"Well, at least he has his own bathroom down here."

"True."

I had to admit that even with the slight weight gain, he was still very attractive and fawn-worthy. He just had to be careful and not overdo it with his sweet obsession, for the sake of his health.

Geoff opened the guestroom door and gave me an overjoyed expression as soon as he saw me. "You're here, Jayden!"

I chuckled. "You didn't know I was coming?"

"No, I've talked on the voice chat with my family."

Sasha shrugged. "Geoff was already chatting when you called."

"We're having special cookies," I said while focusing on Geoff.

"Why they are special?" he asked.

"They have eight specific ingredients, you'll see."

"I'll be back right quick," Sasha said as she walked away. "Just going to the bathroom." She marched up the stairs.

Geoff still gave me his expression of joy, and I had to admit that my presence meaning something to him warmed my heart with a more muted joy. I'd been enjoying his company a bit recently, even despite the awkward moment we'd shared before my forced breakup with Ollie.

"I've told my family about you," Geoff said.

"Aw, really?" That was sweet of him.

"Yah, I've told them that you're my special friend."

I got shy all of a sudden because he knew just how to make me feel as special as he'd told his family I was.

"You're still depressed, Jayden?" Geoff had only a slight frown but kind of a smile as well, probably making sure I was okay.

Ugh, I wished he hadn't brought that up, but I knew he meant well. I tried my hardest to fight any sad feelings over Ollie and angry ones over my suspension, both threatening to come my way. "I hate being suspended. I'll definitely never fight again, though."

"No, fights are not the solutions. I'm sad about your suspension."

"It's okay. I'll live. As for Ollie, it'll probably take a long time to heal, but I'm trying. That's why I'm here. I want to get my mind off everything and just unwind."

"You think that you find a new boyfriend?"

Sometimes, Geoff didn't seem to know what to say and what not to say, and I figured maybe it was a combination of his limited English and direct nature. "I don't think there's anyone else on this island, not that I've been looking. But even if I were looking, I'd most likely have to travel out of the island, because what are the odds of finding another guy who's interested in me?"

"You're so very sad, and you think about those negative things because you don't see the positive things."

I sighed, not wanting to continue the conversation anymore. It was hurting more than it was helping, and I could see from Geoff's genuine care and concern that he was oblivious to my unspoken wishes.

"Jayden?"

"Yeah?"

"If I would be gay, then I'm your boyfriend." Geoff gave me a warm smile.

I let out a soft laugh because it was definitely not what I'd expected to hear. He seriously needed to work more on his English because of the connotation of some of the stuff he said. Still, he could be so adorable at times, and it made me feel good around him. "I like you. You're a good person, and I'm glad we're friends."

That overjoyed expression again, and he threw himself on me with a tight hug. He was starting to spoil me with these hugs, and while it was still awkward for him to do this, I didn't complain at all. My heart didn't even race like it used to whenever he hugged me. In fact, it sort of melted in a way I couldn't explain.

"I like to hold you," he said, "because you're so very warm."

It was nice that a straight guy liked to hug without it having to mean anything non-platonic. Ollie kept trying to creep into my thoughts, but I wanted to shove him aside to allow myself to focus on something that wouldn't test my emotions. I wasn't sure why, but I found myself resting the side of my head against his right shoulder. "Thanks for the hug. I needed one."

"Yah, it feels good. You can ask any time for a hug and I don't say no."

"Aw, thanks. I appreciate that."

"No problems."

Confusion filled my head, and I wasn't sure what to make of the long hug because we were just friends. I supposed I just had to get used to it because there were many more to come. I did like hugs, though. I'd always had.

"Jayden?" He still held me.

"Yeah?"

"You want to stay here and sleep?"

That was a surprising offer, given that Sasha would've normally been the one to ask if I wanted to stay the night. "You mean, tonight?"

"Yah, you can sleep with me on the bed, and we can hug more like special friends."

I wasn't sure if things were quietly escalating into an uncharted territory that I'd never even thought of. We were friends, and he was straight, yet he wanted to give me many hugs, even in bed, which was practically cuddling. A part of me was tempted by the offer because it felt good being in his arms, but another part of me saw a warning sign. What if I ended up developing feelings for him? It'd be one-sided from the start until the end, and I didn't know if I really wanted to take that risk. After all, it wasn't exactly impossible. He looked a lot like Ollie, he had a great voice that soothed me so easily, and he gave some of the best hugs—Ollie was number one in that department.

Then again, maybe staying the night wouldn't be so bad. I didn't want to go back home, anyway, now that there was a chance that Mitch was staying the night. He lived in mainland Michigan, and the last ferry ride there had already left. Thankfully, he didn't visit every day because of his job.

I decided to break the hug because it had lasted long enough, probably almost a minute, but definitely not as long as the one I'd had with Ollie at the state park. I smiled at Geoff, feeling a little relaxed. He'd won without having to try, and that scared me a little. No, but maybe I wouldn't feel anything more for him since the reminder of his being straight continued to ring in my head. That was why staying the night and sharing a bed with him was safe because he wouldn't even be interested in making a move, and I was relieved about that.

"Okay," I said. "I'll stay the night. But I might have to walk or take a carriage taxi back home to get some clothes for tomorrow."

Overjoyed, he said, "I go with you for the company, yah?"

God, why was he so adorable? He reminded me of Ollie

in many ways except with his own charm that was powerful enough to capture my attention. I didn't have to think about Ollie whenever I was around Geoff because Geoff was unique enough to stand out on his own.

I nodded. "Sure, okay, yeah."

"Cool! I want to make you feel good and super happy also."

I chuckled. "You already make me feel good." I wouldn't say I felt *super* happy, at least not in the overjoyed way he was, but I was definitely in a better mood than when I'd been at home. Still, what difference did it make?

Was Geoff blushing all of a sudden? "That's so very nice to say. And happy also?"

I gave him a nod, locking eyes with him in a sudden silence. For the first time since meeting him, I wanted to fall asleep in his arms.

All night long.

Sasha's loud clomps down the stairs startled us and forced Geoff to add extra distance between us. She appeared with an unsuspecting smile and walked past me toward the kitchenette. "Sorry it took long. My mom needed some things she couldn't reach."

"It helps to be tall," I said.

"Yep, and I don't even have to use stepladders."

"I'm staying the night, by the way."

Sasha beamed and clamped her hands together. "Yay!" I knew she'd have that reaction because it'd been a long time since I'd stayed the night here. "You're sleeping on the sofa, right? Because, you know, Geoff has the guestroom."

I gave Geoff a glance and smiled knowingly, and he did

the same. I felt bad because I always told Sasha just about everything unless I was sworn to secrecy like with Ollie the one time and recently Geoff. If I confessed to her about my tiny but confusing feelings for Geoff that made me question what they really were, she might suspect something she shouldn't. Or maybe I was just overthinking it? What was so wrong with telling her how I felt, anyway? Geoff was straight, after all.

I looked back at Sasha and tried to adopt a cool tone to avoid suspicion. If I acted nervous or reluctant, it could cause her to wonder why Geoff would even share the bed with me.

"It's okay. It's not to fear. I sleep with Jayden on the bed. No problems." Oh. Geoff had beaten me to it. That was a relief.

Sasha nodded, and for the first time, she didn't look unfazed like the other times Geoff and I had been around each other. I could see a little twitch on her face, along with a brief expression that told me she had to think for a moment, but she got back to normal. "Okay. Well, it *is* a big bed."

The oven beeped, and she grabbed an oven mitt to get the cookie sheet out. Saved by the beep after such an awkward few seconds. The aroma of the Great Eight cookies seduced me enough to drool, and Geoff and I walked toward the counter where she'd placed the cookie sheet. We each grabbed one, and I was in heaven all over again from just the first bite.

Geoff's overjoyed expression was practically the same as before, but I could tell he liked it. He gave Sasha a thumbs up, so there was that. I could look at his face for a while and just admire him. No, wait, I shouldn't be thinking like this. He wasn't just my friend; he was straight.

Then again, Ollie had been "straight" at one point.

Chapter 20

I opted for a carriage taxi and paid extra for the driver to wait for me by my house as it counted as two rides. The temperature had significantly dropped, and I rode with Geoff next to me on my right side, just the two of us in the back while the driver focused on the road. I slightly shivered in my thick jacket. I probably should've worn a coat, instead.

It was odd how mysterious Sasha had started acting when Geoff and I had announced we were leaving. It was like she'd suspected something, even though nothing had actually been going on between me and Geoff. Well, except for our private hugs and the "if I were X or Y" banter.

"You are cold, Jayden?" he asked.

I nodded while looking at the lush scenery; dusk wasn't too far away.

"We make us warm together with the bodies."

I tried to smile, and he really was adorable and so innocent, not realizing the connotations of a lot of his affections for being a straight guy. Still, if he could keep me warm, I wouldn't complain. "Sure, okay, yeah."

He pulled me into his arms and let me rest my head on

his shoulder, warming me up already. That only made me more confused. He was straight, too affectionate, and bold enough to hold me like this in public when the residents could get the wrong idea. He was also easy to think about in a way I probably shouldn't. It was ironic that he was this publicly affectionate with me for being a straight guy, while Ollie was gay and had never been the type to do it in public, save for the final kiss we'd shared.

Ollie... Why couldn't things just work out for us? Why couldn't he just sneak into Sasha's house and make that our meetup spot? Maybe we would've still been together.

"You like these things, Jayden?"

I snuggled against Geoff, because at this point, he'd made me feel comfortable enough to do so. "Yeah."

"Me also."

That was largely why I was so confused. He enjoyed this, and I couldn't imagine any straight guy wanting to do it with even a platonic female friend, let alone another guy—and with enthusiasm, no less. "Yeah?"

"Yah, it feels good."

A soft moan of comfort slipped out of my mouth, and I realized I had to be careful and not give him the wrong idea.

"Jayden?"

"Yeah?"

"We can hug still on the bed, yah? Tonight?"

How exactly would that be? I'd never done it with anyone, not even Ollie. Geoff would be the first one, and he was just a straight friend. That said, to have a cuddle buddy when I hadn't known they could've existed here was suddenly something I felt I could need. I imagined feeling warm in his arms all night while falling asleep on a bed that was much more comfortable than my own. "Sure, okay, yeah."

"Cool! We have all the night to hug us?"

I chuckled. "I guess we can do that."

What was going on between me and Geoff, anyway? Why were we like this with each other? Sometimes, just sometimes, I wondered what it was like to be romantic with him.

To be his boyfriend.

Geoff and I returned to Sasha's house while I carried my duffel bag, and we went back down into the basement.

She was sitting at the bar table with her laptop in front of her. Her smile wasn't as strong as I'd expected, and it made me wonder what she was thinking. "How was the carriage taxi?" Even her tone seemed a bit off. Was she okay?

I shrugged. "Cold."

"I take these things for you, Jayden." Geoff grabbed my duffel bag with his signature overjoyed expression.

I smiled happily. "Thanks."

"No problems. I make a short call to a good friend in Germany because she doesn't go to sleep yet. Be back!" He rushed toward the guestroom and went inside.

"Jaydles," Sasha whispered with a weird look. "Is there something going on between you guys that I don't know about?" Wow, so she *had* suspected us, after all. "Because number one, he's straight, and number two, the agency he's with doesn't allow any of that. Don't you remember I told you about them being strict about that?"

Ugh, I'd totally forgotten about that stupid policy. "Yeah, I remember. There's nothing going on between us, though, so no worries."

"Good, just making sure, because I don't want him to get in trouble if the agency finds out, which could also affect our chances of having another student someday if we ever wanted another one. We're not getting another one, but just in case."

"Okay, I get it. Why do you ask, anyway?"

"Well, I know he's straight, but even if he wasn't and that the agency was okay with it, I personally don't think it'd be right to do that to Ollie."

"But me and Ollie aren't even together anymore."

"I know, but it's still recent. And besides, you *could* be if he ends up talking to you again and comes up with a plan or something." She really did want us back together.

That only made me frown a bit, and I suddenly missed Ollie a lot. I wished Sasha's hopes were the same as mine, but they weren't. I'd lost hope because there was no way Ollie and I would be able to be together again until college, and that was assuming he'd want me back. What if he ended up swearing off love by then?

"I'm sorry, I shouldn't have brought him up."

"I do miss him, Sash. I do."

"I know, Jaydles."

"But...I want to tell you something." It was finally time to tell her the truth about my confusion toward Geoff. It wasn't like the agency would care about how I felt, anyway, because nothing would ever come out of it.

Sasha sighed. "Please don't tell me you're falling for Geoff." Why was she so sad about it? Besides, it wasn't like it would ever happen.

"I mean, I'm not in *love* with him or anything."

"But you like him?" Why was she so suspicious?

I lowered my eyebrows. "He's straight. He likes girls."

"That wasn't my question." What was with her tonight?

It took me a while to reply, and when I was about to open my mouth, she said, "Look, before you say anything, I'm just going to tell you how I feel about all this. I don't want anything like that happening between you guys, not even if he was gay or if the agency allowed it."

"But why? I mean, it's *obviously* not going to happen, but I'm just curious."

"Because it's weird. He lives here, for one. And the fact that you're going to start sharing a bed makes me hope you stay friends because it'd be rude if you were boyfriends doing that here when you're not even adults yet. I don't mind you sharing a bed *now* because he's straight. And he's also like my new little brother. Plus, he's only fifteen, and you're seventeen, so, yeah."

"Well, to be fair, he'll be sixteen before I turn eighteen."

"Still, I think it'd be pushing it just a little in terms of age gaps between people our age. And then, there's the fact that I'm just not a fan of my best friend dating my foreign exchange student. It makes me uncomfortable. I'm sorry, but I can't help how I feel. Better to be honest about it, you know?"

Confusion filled my head because it made no sense. I was sure it wasn't uncommon for foreign exchange students to date, even if the agencies were strict about it. Why was Sasha acting like that? She was normally much more open-minded, but not in this case, apparently. At this rate, it was a good thing Geoff and I would never be more than friends. I was also relieved she didn't know we'd made plans to cuddle in bed. How would I explain *that*?

And I suddenly didn't want to back out on cuddling with him.

Sasha drew a big breath. "So, now that you know how I feel, can you promise me you'll never be anything more than platonic friends?"

"But that won't happen because he's straight, so what's the point?"

"I know, but just in case, I don't know. You never really know, I guess. Still, just promise me, please?"

Geoff was most likely straight even despite the affectionate way he'd expressed toward me. Besides, why wouldn't he be when he was a strong ally of LGBTQ rights and lived in a very liberal city? I didn't have to make a silly promise over nothing, but it clearly meant a lot to Sasha, and it was an easy promise to make.

I managed a reassuring smile. "Sure, okay, yeah. I promise."

That made her happier, and she immediately started showing me some anime stuff on her laptop, finally back to her normal self.

Yep. An easy promise, indeed.

Chapter 21

Since the fall up north was much colder than in the southern part of Michigan, I usually wore comfy PJs. Because Geoff and I had planned to cuddle all night, I'd decided to wear a T-shirt instead of the PJ top while keeping the bottoms. He dressed the same way, so we matched.

In the guestroom, I flicked off the light and crawled under the sheets and comforter. Geoff had already been lying on the right side of the bed. That was okay. I didn't mind being on the door side.

There was an awkward moment of silence, just the two of us lying on our backs while my heart beat a little faster from the nervousness of sharing a bed with a guy. Geoff broke the ice by turning to his side and wrapping his arm around me, signaling me to turn my back toward his front side, but not too pressed against each other. It was definitely warm, and the cuddle was nice.

"Jayden?" Geoff still chose to speak in a low tone, despite everyone being asleep two floors above us with their bedroom doors closed and no way of hearing us unless we yelled.

I did the same. "Yeah?"

"You feel sometimes alone?"

"You mean lonely?"

"Yah."

Oh, did I. After Ollie had been taken away from me, things weren't the same. I'd finally had the chance to be with a great guy, only for his parents to forbid us to be together, and a mean girl to make sure we'd stay apart. Even though I was still depressed about it in general, I realized I'd been better in the evening and at night after being close to Geoff. Of course, it didn't mean it would last, but I clung onto hope that the pain would eventually fade away.

"Yeah," I muttered.

"Me also."

"You asked me earlier if I wanted to find a new boyfriend. What about you? Have you thought about finding a new girlfriend?"

"I don't know, Jayden. I've dated three girls but they don't want me. Two are cisgender and one is transgender, and they are pretty and nice, but I can't give them what they want."

I didn't have to see his face to know he was frowning. I was, too, and the two of us could relate in ways we probably hadn't thought before. Then again, I was surprised about one of his exes being trans, and it showed how supportive he was for a cisgender straight guy. "I know how you feel."

God, I needed this cuddle. I'd never imagined how nice and comfortable it'd be. The fact that it would happen all night made me smile like a dork. While I missed Ollie and wished I could have him back in my life, I had Geoff. Granted, I didn't have him in the same way, but I still had him in my life, and our friendship had been growing stronger. I cared about him, and I knew he cared about me.

"I don't understand. You're beautiful, Jayden. I think, that a good boy is lucky to be your boyfriend."

"Aw, Geoff, you're sweet." But, admittedly, that was not a very straight male thing to say.

"I tell you the truth."

"Thanks. I don't think I'm beautiful, but still…thanks."

"You see something that I don't see in the mirror. I think, that you see a ugly face, I don't know. But I don't see a ugly face. I see a beautiful face."

I wasn't sure why I turned around, but I did. I looked at him with very little distance between our faces, my heartrate speeding up from being too close to him. His soft breath warmed my lips. God, why did he have to be straight? Why couldn't I find someone like him if I couldn't be with Ollie? Even despite the continual weight gain from all that junk he refused to stop eating, he was so attractive, so awesome as a person, so honest and easy to trust, and he made me feel beautiful. The best part was that he seemed like he would've been openly affectionate in public if he were gay. He'd dipped his toes in the pool of courage just by holding me in the carriage taxi. It wasn't like there hadn't been people around, yet he'd done it.

"You're so good-looking," I said with a smile. "Very attractive."

"Yah?"

"Yeah."

After a pause, he asked, "You think ever about me?"

It took me a moment to answer because it wasn't a question I'd expected from a straight guy. "All the time."

"Me also."

"Yeah?"

"Yah."

I didn't know what to make of that. A part of me did wonder about him really being straight, but the other part of me insisted he was, because it would only complicate things and affect our friendship.

"Jayden?"

"Yeah?"

"I'm not gay."

My heart stopped, and I immediately wondered if I'd been obvious in any way that would have him feel like I'd been coming onto him when I hadn't meant to at all.

"But I'm not straight also."

My jaw almost dropped, and my tongue was paralyzed. Wow, I had no idea what to say to *that* admission. He wasn't supposed to be straight! Being straight meant a smooth friendship.

"I have thought that I was straight because I don't think about boys, and I've had only girlfriends and not boyfriends. But then I've met you and I think always about you."

Oh, Geoff. His admission suddenly challenged everything. I'd even made a promise to Sasha that nothing would ever happen between us because I'd been convinced things between me and Geoff could never evolve into something more.

I'd been wrong. Or maybe I didn't want to accept it as right. I didn't need the complication that was practically guaranteed.

"I've made research online, Jayden, because I've wanted to know what I am. I think, that I'm panromantic because I don't care what the person is, what the gender is or no gender. I'm not bothered by those things, only that the person has a good heart."

I wasn't sure why that didn't surprise me, and it was nice to hear. But panromantic? Didn't he mean pansexual since he was most likely not asexual? That was oddly specific.

"Jayden?"

"Yeah?"

"I think, that you like me not only as a friend, yah?"

Did I? I loved Ollie, though. I was getting more and more confused by the second, and I still couldn't say much. This was exactly why Geoff was supposed to be straight, and it was also why I realized I hadn't wanted to believe he wasn't all along.

"Because I like you as more than only a friend, and I want to know what feeling it is to kiss a boy."

The more he kept that up, the more I wondered if I really did like him more than I wanted to admit. Ugh, why couldn't he just be straight?

"Can I kiss you, Jayden?"

Oh, Geoff… Why? Why did he have to develop feelings for me? Then again, I'd thought about it myself and had wondered what it was like to share a kiss with him. Our faces were too close as it was, and we were almost there.

"Geoff…" I whispered, my heart starting to melt while my brain tried to tackle the confusion.

"Yah?"

"I don't know what to do about this."

"I don't know also. But I know, that I want to kiss you."

I had to admit that I wanted to kiss him too. The entire time, nothing between us had any sexual undertones, which made me feel safe. No electricity that apparently went straight to one's penis just by looking at a guy, no hormones or hunger by even being near a guy… Simply heart-related over someone special, the desire to love and be loved with so much romantic affection to compliment it. Allosexual people, being the opposite of asexual, didn't understand us because whatever romantic desire they experienced was tied to their sexual feelings.

Tonight made me realize I'd just gotten a new opportunity with someone else, someone other than Ollie. I still missed him. I still wanted him, and I'd honestly do whatever I could to have him back in my life. It was over, though.

Geoff sighed. "But if you would not want to kiss me, then I don't kiss you. It's okay. It's not to fear. I understand that you don't feel comfortable about that. No problems."

"I do, Geoff, I do want to kiss you." Wow, that had slipped without me even thinking clearly. "But what about the agency? Aren't they strict about these things?"

"Those persons don't need to know nothing. It's our secret, yah?" He had a point because it wasn't like the agency would ever find out. How would they when no one would even know anything about us?

"But what about Sasha?" I asked. "She doesn't want us to be more than just friends."

Geoff didn't say anything for a while, just staring at me. "She won't know. It's a secret." Then, he grew bolder and placed his lips over mine, and he got partially on top of me to continue.

The kiss was soft and warm, and it melted my insides. When he slipped his tongue inside my mouth, just the way Kail had done many times, I tried to close it a little to chasten up the kiss from getting too passionate. I didn't want passion, not that I knew how to show that. Passion led to sex, especially when on a bed and in the dark, and I didn't want to have sex. For the rest of my life, if possible.

Geoff definitely enjoyed himself. But just how excited was he from his hungry kisses? The possibility of being horny only made me feel uncomfortable, and I wasn't sure if he'd be tempted to want to take things further than I didn't want. If only we could just kiss and nothing more, but I couldn't be sure if that was all he wanted.

I broke the kiss and tried to smile. "Geoff...I don't want to have sex."

"I don't want sex also, Jayden. I want only to kiss. We kiss again?"

I had to admit that that instantly made me feel safe. So, he really was a good guy, after all. It made sense because he hadn't shown any sexual interest the entire time. I might've been oblivious to many signs, like flirting, but I knew horny moods all too well, thanks to Kail, and even Mitch toward Mom. Now, it made me want Geoff more than ever. "Sure, okay, yeah."

We gave each other more kisses, and while I preferred tongueless kissing, I rested assured I could let him make out with me because it wouldn't go beyond that. His frontside down below wasn't even close to mine, which was awesome.

I still had mixed emotions, though, and I suddenly missed Ollie more. I liked Geoff, but I loved Ollie. I knew I had every right to kiss anyone I wanted because Ollie and I weren't together anymore, but the guilt continued to linger.

This time, it was Geoff who broke the kiss, and he looked at me for a moment, sighing. "Thank you for those sweet kisses. They were so very special, and you're now more special to me." He got off me and wrapped his arm around my body, guiding me to turn to my side so that my back faced him. "Goodnight, Jayden."

"Night, Geoff." What a confusing moment. After minutes of being lost in thought, Geoff's light snoring filled my ears. As good and warm as it felt to be in his arms, I couldn't sleep. I had two issues boggling inside my head that threatened to send me into another depression. The first was that I'd made out with someone other than Ollie, and it made me feel so guilty about it because of my strong feelings for him that refused to go away. The other more important issue was bigger and made me more upset with myself. I'd broken my promise to Sasha.

I'd betrayed her.

Chapter 22

Almost a whole week had passed, and it was Thursday. The guilt and depression were so strong that I'd isolated myself from everyone most of that time, not that I'd been able to go back to school until today. I knew I had to be careful to avoid any suspicions from Sasha, so I feigned being busier with school than ever. Given that I had average grades, it was believable, at least.

Then, there was Geoff. He'd already been awake by the time I'd woken up, and it was like it hadn't happened. It'd been the last time I'd seen him, but we did chat a lot on the app—not a single mention of our kisses.

I closed my locker and headed toward the administration wing to drop off the essay. Finally! Ugh, what an agonizing chore that had taken forever for me to finish. Never again! I walked inside Principal Olsen's office, but she wasn't here, so I set it on the mail tray for her to check later.

I decided to check on the signup sheet for the LGBTQ support group proposal that was still taped on the wall by the counselor's office. I groaned at just the five signatures, mine and Sasha's still being the last ones. At this rate, it was never going to happen.

"Jayden?" Mrs. Calder called from her office. She was usually busy as the school counselor, but right now she had no one there.

Reluctantly, I walked inside and stopped in front of her desk, managing a little smile. "Hi, Mrs. Calder."

"I see that you signed up for the LGBTQ support group proposal on the first day of school." She gave me a warm smile, always a sweetheart from what I remembered. She'd been here for decades, probably a senior citizen. "Could you close the door and take a seat, please? I'd like to talk to you for a moment."

I nodded and closed the door, then sat down on one of the chairs, pulling it closer to her desk. "I'm not in trouble, am I?"

"Oh, no, no. I did hear about your suspension, of course."

I wasn't surprised. Then again, she probably had to know, what with being the school counselor. "I learned my lesson, don't worry."

"Good, I'm glad to hear that. I hope you stay out of trouble from now on because you've always been a nice and quiet boy. I don't want to see you change for the worse." She did look concerned, at least.

I gave her a nod, not really knowing what exactly to say. I'd never talked to her much, just a few times about school-related stuff.

"So? Anything going on in your life that you'd like to talk about?"

"Does this have to do with the suspension?"

"Kind of. Principal Olsen told me to have a talk with you while you were suspended. I was actually going to send you an email asking if you could see me soon, but I happened to see you around, so that worked out."

"Oh, okay."

"Was there anything that triggered you to push Gracie against the lockers? Anything specific that might've caused your anger?"

I didn't want to have to get into it, but it seemed like I would've had to at some point. Unfortunately, everyone who wasn't my friend believed I pushed Gracie. "I hate her," I muttered.

Mrs. Calder acknowledged me with a nod. "I see. Hate is a strong word, Jayden. Is there a specific reason why you might feel that way about her? Did she maybe say or do something to you to trigger a response like that?"

I shrugged. "She never liked me."

"Why do you think that is?"

"She actually told me. Apparently, she's had this major crush on...a guy."

"Oliver Belasco, right?"

What? How did Mrs. Calder know it was Ollie? Unless Principal Olsen had told her? Ugh, she probably knew everything. "Yeah...that's him."

"Do you think she felt threatened in some way?"

"Yep, because Ollie has feelings for me, but I didn't know at the time. I think she suspected and that could be why she didn't like me. Over the summer, me and Ollie reunited and got closer. We eventually became boyfriends and that pissed her off, so she told his dad who then forced us to break up."

Mrs. Calder nodded, still looking concerned. "I see. I'm sorry to hear that, Jayden. I'm sure he meant a lot to you."

"I loved him, and he loved me. We still love each other, but...whatever. Life goes on, right?" Of course, it didn't feel like it. Now that we'd been talking about Ollie, it made me miss him so much. Despite what Geoff and I had done and how we felt about each other, I'd break it off if Ollie came back into the picture, not that Geoff and I had repeated anything.

"Thankfully, life does go on, and you'll eventually heal. I know it doesn't feel that way right now, but it will. It takes time." She tried to smile.

I was definitely not going to tell her about Geoff. He'd confided in me, and I didn't want to betray his trust. If only I hadn't betrayed Sasha in the process.

"I'm going to email you some resources. Some of them deal with anger issues, others with coping skills, and I also have LGBTQ support sites to link you to. I think you'll find these helpful."

I was probably not going to read any of them, but I didn't have a choice. She could send away for all I cared. I just wanted to get out of this island and never come back. I wanted to be somewhere warm where I could be myself more without being judged for it. An LGBTQ city would be ideal, but they tended to be more expensive.

I wished I could take Ollie with me, or Geoff, if Ollie couldn't come. What would happen between me and Geoff, anyway? Had our kisses affected our friendship? We chatted a lot every day, but how would it be in person? Would it be any different? I loved Ollie, but I liked Geoff. I missed Ollie, but I felt weird about things between me and Geoff going back to before the kisses, before the affection. I hadn't just gotten used to them, but they meant something to me.

Ugh, why was I so confused?

At lunch period, I carried my tray to our usual table, and Sasha beamed, even though we'd already seen each other today. Geoff's overjoyed expression gave me hope, though. I didn't want us to go back to normal, despite knowing it was probably for the best, but I suddenly missed being close to him.

"I'm so glad you're back today," Sasha said.

"Yah, welcome back!" Geoff added.

"Did you turn your essay in yet?"

"Yeah," I said. "And Mrs. Calder wanted a talk with me. I didn't know that was part of the suspension since Principal Olsen didn't mention anything about that."

"Oh. How did *that* go?"

I shrugged. "Not too bad, actually. I mean, Mrs. Calder has always been pretty nice. It also wasn't a long conversation, though."

"That's good, at least. Well, *I've* been trying to get Geoff into anime, but it's not working out like I hoped." She formed a dramatic pout.

"I'm sorry," Geoff said. "I don't like animes. Some are okay but not much of them."

I smiled at him. "Looks like we have another thing in common."

"You don't like animes?"

"Some."

Sasha tittered. "You like a *little* more than some, Jayden. Don't even try that."

I shrugged. "You're the obsessive fan here."

"And proud of it. Anime's life." She grabbed her phone. "Okay, music time." She fiddled with it and turned on some K-pop at a low volume. She was probably browsing the internet from how focused she was.

Geoff grabbed his phone and began typing something.

My phone chimed with a text notification, and I knew it was him from the app's unique sound. I grabbed it and checked the message.

Geoff: *I need to talk please to you. Hallway?*

I looked at him and gave him a nod. I got up from my seat, not even feeling hungry anymore. What could it be that he wanted to talk to me about? I hoped it wasn't anything bad because I didn't need to deal with extra drama in my life. "I'm going to the bathroom, guys, I'll be back."

Geoff got up too. "I go to the toilet also. Be back!"

Sasha let out a dramatic sigh while still focused on her phone. "Hurry up, then. I don't want to be alone for too long." She wasn't upset, though.

"Yes, Mistress." I led the way and reached the narrow hallway, then turned to my immediate left to move away from the open door to the cafeteria. Thankfully, no one was around, but I still chose to speak in a low tone. "Hey, what's going on?"

Geoff frowned, and I hoped it wasn't something I didn't want to hear. I needed some good news for once. "I don't stop to think about you."

Oh? So, he really did want something? Maybe? "I feel the same way. I enjoyed our kisses."

There was his overjoyed expression again, and I liked seeing him that way. "When I stand up from the bed on the day that we were with us, I've feared that Sasha come down to see us. And on those other days of this week when I and Sasha have talked with us, she was with me always. I don't have much privacies."

I wasn't sure what Geoff was trying to say. "You mean…you wanted to talk to me about the kisses?"

"Yah. I miss you, Jayden."

My heart flittered in a flash, making me blush hard. "Aw, I miss you too."

"I want to kiss you more times."

So, things had been normal all this time. I'd just assumed otherwise. As much as I didn't want to be confused anymore, as much as I betrayed Sasha, fighting my romantic desire for Geoff was becoming more and more challenging. It wasn't fair that she'd made me promise not to get involved with him. Why couldn't she accept it? What if he could make me happy? I enjoyed his company, and I'd gotten spoiled with his affection. Given that I wanted more kisses from him, I'd say I was spoiled with those too.

"I want that, too, but how?"

A frown spanned Geoff's face. "I know. It's so very difficult to be with you alone. I don't chat with you how I want because Sasha can see sometimes my handy."

I'd always known she was nosy, but I sometimes wondered if she was especially so with him because of any suspicions. Unless I was overthinking it? It wasn't always easy to tell with Geoff's limited English. He could say one thing but mean something else. Nuances really did matter.

"And your house? You have much privacies in there?"

I'd never invited anyone to my house before. Sasha had never once entered because she'd been afraid of second-hand smoke. She knew my house was smoky and couldn't be in that environment. It suddenly worked out in my favor, now that I'd met Geoff.

I gave him a reassuring smile. "I do. But I should warn you. My mom smokes a lot inside the house."

"It's okay. It's not to fear. I don't smoke but my mum and my dad smoke sometimes. No problems."

"Then, maybe you can come over this weekend? You can just tell Sasha you're going out for a long walk to show your family parts of the island."

Geoff's face lit up more. "Cool!"

What was it about him? Where were we headed with our friendship? It was a risk because I knew myself all too well. I'd eventually fall for him like I'd done with Kail and Ollie. Why would Geoff be any different when he made a great boyfriend? It would just have to be our little secret.

No one would ever know.

Chapter 23

On Friday evening, I rode home on a carriage taxi from the general store while holding a grocery bag in each hand. I was giddy because I'd get to see Geoff for what could be an awesome hangout in my room, no restrictions. I'd even bought him a case of root beer to go with the can of whipped cream—*not* the can with "BEDROOM ONLY!" on a sticky note—and bottle of candy sprinkles that had already been in the kitchen.

I loved hanging out with Sasha, but ever since she'd spoken her upsetting truth about the idea of me and Geoff, I'd been left with no choice but to hang out with him in secret. I hated lying to her because it sucked, but after sharing a special and romantic moment with Geoff, there was no way I'd be able to go back to being just friends with him. Maybe I was selfish, but my feelings for him continued to grow. We'd chatted for hours last night because he'd feigned being tired early and had used the extra time to spend with me on the chat app, just messaging away.

Sadly, we didn't have all night because Geoff wasn't allowed to stay out too late, especially because Sasha's parents were responsible for him. He'd told her he wanted to go out alone for a long walk to spend personal time with his family through video chat while showing them parts of the island.

My phone chimed with a text notification, and I checked it to see that it was from the secret lesbian. She announced that her parents had found tons of lesbian media on her phone after checking their phone records. My mouth dropped open, and I immediately wanted to hug her. They were sending her away soon to live with even stricter religious relatives in the Upper Peninsula near the Wisconsin border, which had to be about seven hours west. So far away and a worse situation for her. At this rate, I'd probably never hear from her again, but just in case, I quickly gave her my home address and told her to email it to herself to save it as an emergency contact. I highly doubted it would work, but it was worth a try.

The carriage taxi came to a stop in front of my house, and I tipped the driver and got out. I rushed to the front door to escape the strong chill, and I shut it with a *brrr*. I scanned the living room, and my eyebrows rose high.

Spotless, and even more so than I'd ever kept it.

I twisted my lips in confusion and marched into the kitchen, only to be welcomed with the strong but great smell of chicken soup. But the most shocking of it all? Mom was attempting to cook, and in new clothes. I set the grocery bags on the table.

She glanced at me, dressed far more nicely than her former tacky clothes that she'd called "comfortable." Now, she wore a simple top with a nice pair of slim-fit jeans I'd never seen her wear before. Even her dyed-blond hair was brushed from root to tip and recently retouched. "Hey." Her tone was always raspy from having smoked most of her life, which was the only thing she couldn't fix. "How are you, sweetie?"

My mouth almost dropped. "Sweetie?" I unzipped my jacket but left it on.

"You're my son, aren't you?"

"Yeah, but…" I studied her for a moment longer. "You're…different. Your hair's not a mess. Your clothes are nicer. You seem happy for being sober. What's…gotten into you?"

She closed the lid of the pot and turned one of the knobs of the stove to let the soup simmer. She let out a deep breath, and her face might as well have glowed. "Mitch happened."

Question marks floated above my head. "Are you high again?" I knew she wasn't.

She pursed her lips with clear frustration. "I'm *trying* to change. Can you at *least* cut me some slack, please?"

"Okay, okay, that's good, but…what does *Mitch* have to do with anything?" I suddenly heard the shower running. "And why is he always here every weekend?"

Mom paused, glancing at the pot. Then, she looked at me. "He's a truck driver. He makes *very* good money."

"Sure, okay, yeah. You told me that already. But…*why* is he always *here*? Doesn't he have his own *place*?"

She paused for a few long seconds and let out a deep breath. "He moved in today."

My mouth dropped wide open. How dare Mom allow

a disgusting swine to move into our home! How dare *any* man be allowed to live here! It was a miracle the retired sex worker actually showered after I'd discovered his gross manners. If only he could just leave and never come back.

"I know you don't like him, Jayden, but—"

I scoffed, shaking my head. "He's a loser, Mom!"

"Hey! *Watch* it." She shot me a set of murderous eyes. "He's a *good* man. You just have to get to know him. And I don't want to hear any more insults coming out of your mouth, you hear me?"

I firmly pressed my lips together. Then, I stormed away and rushed into my room, slamming the door shut. I kicked a few articles of clothing strewn all over the floor to get them out of the way. I lay on the bed on my side and hugged my pillow. Why did I hate Mitch so much? Sure, he'd tried to befriend me with kindness, but that didn't mean he was welcome as a permanent household member. I wasn't ready to accept him. I wasn't ready to accept *any* man for Mom.

My phone chimed with the chat app's sound, and I was relieved it was Geoff. Was he here already? I grabbed my phone from my jeans pocket and read his message.

Geoff: *I'm now here! You can open please the door for me? It's cold! :)*

I jolted out of bed and frantically cleaned up my room as much possible, mostly the clothes that were on the floor. I hadn't realized he'd be here so quickly, not that I wasn't happy to see him. He must've been on a carriage taxi around the same time I'd been on mine. I had just seconds to make my room look presentable if I didn't want to keep him waiting out in the cold. Ugh, but I hadn't gotten the chance to vacuum the carpet in my room. It wasn't too bad, but still.

After finishing with my room, I left and opened the front door. As soon as I saw Geoff looking as adorably overjoyed as ever, my heart thawed from the bitterness of being stuck with Mitch. "Come in." I couldn't control the rising happiness from his existence.

Mom peeked out from the kitchen straight ahead and formed a polite smile. "I didn't know we were having company. Who's this, Jayden?" She was at least calm from being offended earlier.

"This is Geoff, a good friend of mine and Sasha's. He's a foreign exchange student from Germany and he's living with Sasha's family while he's here." I smiled at him but tried not to be obvious, since Mom wasn't stupid.

"Hey, Geoff, welcome to America."

"Thank you," he said. "Hello to you also, Jayden's mum." He waved.

Mom let out a raspy chuckle. "Just call me Marsha."

"Ah. Okay, I call you now Marsha."

"So, Germany, huh? Wow. How do you like it here so far?"

"I really much like it! Of course, it's so very different in Germany, but I like my times here also and I want to see more things."

Mom smiled warmly. "Well, that's good to hear. How long are you here for?"

"I go back to Germany on December."

December. How I'd totally forgotten because it hadn't

been a huge deal until now. That word suddenly made me sad. Would I ever get to see him again after he left?

"Are you hungry, Geoff?" Mom asked. "I just made some chicken soup and there's plenty. Come and eat if you'd like."

"Yah, okay, thank you. Chicken soup is yummy."

Mom smiled and went back into the kitchen.

I suppressed a groan because it meant we'd have to join Mom and Mitch at the kitchen table. We didn't have a dining room to justify eating in separate rooms, and I wasn't a fan of eating dinner in my room because of possible pests. Oh, well. I'd get over it.

As I led Geoff to the kitchen, the bathroom door to our left opened. Mitch stepped out looking clean, for once. He had on a freshly laundered tank top and decent jeans. Even his brown hair was brushed, but because it was long and loose at the moment, along with a trimmed goatee, he looked like Jesus.

Mom gave me a knowing smile. "Jayden, aren't you going to introduce him?"

Ugh, Mom, really? That was *definitely* intentional, but I didn't have a choice if I didn't want to come across as a jerk. I slapped on my fakest smile but didn't look much at Mitch. "Geoff, this is Mitch, my mom's boyfriend."

Mitch extended a hand for a shake, forming a warm expression. "How are you, Geoff?" His deep and hoarse voice sounded extra polite.

"Good, and you?"

"Great. Starving, if I must say." He let out a deep chuckle and headed toward the table.

I grabbed the grocery bags and put them on the counter to be stocked later. I took a seat next to Geoff and across from Mitch while Mom grabbed four bowls from the cupboard. What a challenge to hide my true feelings and put on the most uncomfortable act. I hadn't realized Mom would've offered Geoff dinner, which cut into my private time with him.

"Mitch, Geoff is from Germany," Mom said while pouring some soup into each bowl. "He's here as a foreign exchange student staying at Sasha's." It was weird to see her social in a normal way. It was what I'd wanted to see for so long, but why did it have to take a man to do it? Why couldn't she have done it on her own?

Mitch's face lit up. "Oh, that's great. Wie ist Deutschland und ist Amerika bisher ein gutes Land?"

What…? Mitch spoke German?

Geoff looked impressed. "Germany is so very nice and beautiful, and America is those things too."

They briefly chatted in German, making me wish I knew what they were saying.

"Mom, did you know Mitch spoke German?" I asked.

"Of course, silly. I know everything about him. It's called getting to know someone. You should try it sometime." She smirked.

I glanced at Mitch who smiled warmly at me, making me feel confused. Ugh, I hated him, and I wanted him gone. Why couldn't he just leave and never come back? And why did he have to make things worse by being so kind and likable? It was like he was intentionally taking away every reason for me to hate him.

Mom handed each of us a bowl, then grabbed hers and took a seat next to Mitch. We began eating.

"Soup's delicious, Marsha," Mitch said as if in heaven.

"Yah, it's yummy," Geoff said. "Thank you."

Mitch smirked. "Don't you mean, danke?"

"Jah, danke." Geoff smiled and continued eating.

I formed a tiny expression that was supposed to be like theirs, except it was weak because of the awkward dinner. I wasn't even that hungry, but I tried my hardest to eat some of the soup.

"Well, I'm glad," Mom said in relief. "It's one of the few meals I can actually make and have it be tasty."

There was a moment of awkward silence while we ate, the only sounds being our slurping.

"So, Geoff, how long are you here for?" Mitch asked.

"I stay here until December and then I go back to Germany."

It hit me again, and I knew I had to mask the sad face that was itching to form. Ever since Geoff and I had gotten closer, particularly in a romantic way, I couldn't stop thinking about the reality. I tried to shove the thoughts aside and focus on dinner and the conversation.

We were done eating, which included more chats between Geoff and Mitch, and the occasional comment from Mom.

"Want to see my room, Geoff?" I asked impatiently.

"Yah, okay."

"Have fun," Mom said with a knowing smirk. She didn't even know I was asexual, since I'd never come out to her. She probably thought Geoff and I were going to have sex, not that she cared whether or not we did. As long as I didn't steal her cigarettes or personally disrespect her, it was all good.

I led Geoff out of the kitchen and into the living room, and we entered my room. Sadly, because of all that time spent with Mom and Mitch, I didn't have much time left with him for the night.

"Cool!" Geoff was way too overjoyed over my room. "There are much pastel colors. You really much like pastels, yah?"

"I do, but I thought about redesigning my room when I can afford it."

"Ah."

Seeing him stand there not only made me melt, but it saddened me all over again as I was reminded he was leaving on New Year's Eve. It was a big reason I didn't dare to be his boyfriend if he ever wanted that title. Given that he was only fifteen, he had at least another couple of years in Germany before he'd be able to do what he wanted as an adult, which could include coming here or me possibly going over there if I ever had the money.

"Jayden, you are now sad?" A hint of a frown spread across Geoff's face.

I strengthened my smile into a tight one, but it didn't feel genuine. I didn't want to kill the mood for either of us. I wanted to make the best of what little time I had left with him. "Can you hold me, Geoff?"

By his reaction, I could tell he melted, exuding the same dreaminess I felt. He stepped closer and wrapped his arms around me for an embrace. As we looked at each other for a moment, our lips touched, and we made out for a long time. I didn't want to let him go. I wanted him to stay the night with me so that I could fall asleep in his arms, cuddling all night.

We stopped but still held each other, and Geoff sighed. "I like you more, Jayden."

"What do you mean?" I kind of had a feeling but wanted to make sure.

"I don't know how I say that, but I like you more than when we've kissed us the first time."

Was he falling for me? I'd suspected something, but I hadn't imagined how deeply he felt. It only ached me more because of the reality, and I knew I wasn't that far behind him when it came to love. It hit me, though. I couldn't hide my sadness over it, and my eyes flooded the longer I stared at him.

"Aw, why you cry, Jayden? Please, don't cry."

"Why does…why does every time I want to be with a guy…something has to happen to work against it?" First Kail because it'd been romantically one-sided, and he'd never wanted anything serious and had turned out to be poison. Then Ollie, someone I still could've been with had it not been for Gracie. He was the real love of my life who continued to dominate my thoughts. Finally, Geoff, and he was leaving on New Year's Eve. Why? Why bother with love when I couldn't seem to have it?

"Give me only one moment, yah?" Geoff said in a deeply sad tone, grabbing his phone. While he wasn't a crybaby like I was, I knew he felt the same way. He called someone, and they answered. "Hi, Sasha… I know, but it has got so very cold and I'm now on Jayden's house... Yah, I know, but I was in the near of his house and then I've stopped to warm me here... Yah, I'm now fine... I know... Yah, I know... Okay... Goodnight also." He ended the call and put it back inside his pocket. "I stay now with you. You're sad and I don't want you to be sad, so I stay to be with you."

Geoff always knew how to touch me in all the right ways, and he suddenly made my night.

"Your mum is okay if I would stay?" he asked.

I wiped my tears and sniffled. "Oh, yeah, totally. She's very liberal and doesn't care about any of that."

He grinned. "We can hug on the bed also?"

I chuckled, my mood brightening at the idea of cuddling with him. "Yep."

"All the night?"

"All night. But...I don't have anything to sleep with that might fit you."

"It's okay. It's not to fear. I take off my shirt and my jeans also, and I sleep with my underwear. No problems."

Uh-oh. I wasn't sure about *that*. It wasn't so much that he'd be almost naked, but more so that he could end up feeling aroused and in the mood. Or maybe I was overthinking it? I knew it'd be uncomfortable to sleep in clothes, and I didn't have anything for him to wear.

Unless...

Ugh, Mitch. He'd definitely have something for Geoff that could fit, but that would mean I'd have to actually talk to him. I wasn't doing that. I didn't want to interact with him again.

"You sleep with your underwear also?" Geoff asked. It was funny how nonsexual it seemed to be for him, and that gave me hope. He didn't seem horny at all. I wanted to trust him.

I lifted just one corner of my mouth. "I'm just…I'm worried."

"Why?" He seemed so oblivious too.

"I don't want to have sex."

"Jayden…" He frowned. "You think, that I'm a horny and dirty boy? Why? I don't think never about those sex things."

Ugh, why had I been so stupid to assume the worst, and I'd probably ended up hurting his feelings over it. He really was great for me, more than I'd thought. The fact that we'd sleep in our underwear together with no chance of sex, on top of him not wanting sex on our first night together, made me see him in a new light. In a way, I sort of wondered if he was asexual, too, but what were the odds of *that* being the case. Maybe he just had a low sex drive? Or maybe he was just that respectful but could eventually want sex later on?

"I'm sorry, Geoff. I shouldn't have made that assumption. I'll sleep in my underwear too."

He smiled a little and held me. "When I stay on the next time, I have a pajama with me, yah?"

I definitely liked that idea a lot. "Deal."

We kissed some more. I knew I shouldn't have been doing this with him. It wasn't just because it was a risk with his leaving, but it meant I had to keep lying to Sasha. My heart couldn't help how it felt, and neither could Geoff's.

The more she forbade me to be with him, the more I wanted to be with him. I had him all to myself tonight, a night of romance and affection and cuddles.

And no one would take that away from me.

Chapter 24

The morning sunlight woke me up on Saturday. I gently moaned while feeling Geoff's arm around me, his bare chest against my naked back, creating more warmth. I still remembered seeing his body that was in decent shape and nice to look at. He wasn't as athletically built as Ollie, though, especially not with consuming all that junk. He had an average build, maybe normal weight.

I'd slept with a guy again, and for the first time in our underwear. Granted, he wore loose boxer shorts, which made me feel a little better. Still, I couldn't believe how far I'd gone because of my feelings for him. No sex at all, just a special connection that no one could seem to come between.

I wasn't over Ollie, though. It was just easier to be distracted by my feelings for Geoff. Sometimes, I wished I could have them both because I didn't want to have to keep juggling between them in my head, but I knew it was forever done with Ollie. Why bother with any hope for him? Then again, any kind of hope for something with Geoff was pointless as long as he was still leaving on New Year's Eve.

Tender kisses tickled my shoulder and the nape of my

neck, and we giggled. I controlled a grimace after smelling a bit of his morning breath from his kisses, something I'd have to get used to if we were to continue sharing a bed. I didn't dare to turn around and risk letting him smell mine.

"You can look here, Jayden?" he asked.

"*Nooo*...my breath!" I chuckled.

"So? It's okay. It's not to fear. I don't care about those silly rules because a kiss is only a kiss. No problems."

But *I* cared. Ugh, I felt defeated because I wanted to see him but didn't want to experience that right now. Still, I turned around and tightly shut my mouth, but he placed his mouth on mine until I opened it and let him kiss me. Okay, so it wasn't too bad, but I preferred it if we at least sucked on some mints if we couldn't brush our teeth right away. I made a mental note to get a pack for the next time.

As soon as his excitement grew and his kisses got hungrier, I broke the kiss. I tried hard not to freak out, even though he'd never expressed any desire to have sex. I turned to lie on my back and looked at the ceiling.

Geoff did the same and sighed. "I'm sorry, Jayden. I really much like to kiss you."

"It's okay, I get it. You can't help yourself sometimes." I'd never be upset over that, at least not with him, because I trusted his intentions. I just wished it never had to be the case because it served as a reminder of our sexualities clashing.

"Jayden?"

"Yeah?"

"You want never to make sex, yah?"

I should've known that topic would've eventually come,

just not so soon. Still, it was my chance to be honest with him to avoid leading him on. *Had* I been leading him on, though? I didn't try to at all. It took me a while to respond. "No, Geoff. I don't want to have sex. Ever."

He let out a deep breath that surprised me by sounding more relieved than disappointed. "You are asexual?"

The moment of truth had finally come, and I was ready to come out and say it. It was weird that I'd never come out to Ollie about it, but it was only because we'd never really brought it up, aside from the one time about his torn views on homosexuality. "Yeah. I'm asexual. And I'm sorry. I *really* am, and I totally understand if it's a problem—"

He turned over to me and wrapped his arm around my chest. "No, no, Jayden, it's okay! It's not to fear. I'm not angry because I'm asexual also. No problems."

Oh? Wow! That was definitely not what I'd expected to hear. It suddenly made sense why he never seemed sexual and that it'd been all in my paranoid head. "Really?"

"Yah. I have the hand, but it's sometimes every year. It's never much times."

Aw, what a great guy. He didn't even sound disappointed, and when I glanced at his face, it was the same expression. I felt like I'd lucked out all of a sudden because it wasn't a common thing for most aces. It put a big smile on my face. "I masturbate more than you do."

"Yah?"

"Yep. I do it because of the pressure that builds up, and it just bothers me each time. The relief feels great, though."

"Same, but I don't feel always that way. I wish, that I don't make those masturbations because I don't like it, but

I have sometimes those pressures also. Yah, okay, so it feels good to make those masturbations, but it's messy and sticky." He shuddered with a grimace spanning his face.

I giggled. "You're silly. So…do you watch…naughty videos? You know, when you masturbate? I do, but I mean, it's the soft kind. No oral or anal."

"I see never those things. Not gay, not straight, not bi, nothing of those." Geoff formed a sour face. "I don't like it, Jayden. Sex to me is yucky, and some of those acts that the persons make are not clean. I don't like even to see the penis or the vagina or the butt. But the breasts are okay, I think, and I like the boy chest also."

I was shocked yet again. How ironic that I'd been the more anxious one of the two when it came to sex, yet all this time, he'd been the one to find sex and sexual organs gross, while I was pretty much sex-indifferent but with no interest in the act itself. That explained why he was fine with sleeping in underwear because it didn't show anything private. When he'd been physically excited a moment ago, it had most likely been a natural bodily response from the friction of our bodies, or so I'd read about online.

"Have you ever had sex?" I asked.

Geoff made another sour face. "Nooo, never! I've not made sex, and if I would not find a person like me that don't want sex, then I'm alone forever with no problems."

So, he really was sex-repulsed.

"And you, Jayden? You've made sex? And please, I don't want the yucky details. Only 'yes' or 'no.'"

That question triggered the thought of Kail and his repulsive face I used to swoon over. I remembered when we'd first had sex and how he'd insisted it was the way to his heart if I did it enough times. That had obviously never happened, and he'd just used me to get off like the fool I'd been. The act itself, me going down on him, hadn't really made me feel the way Geoff definitely would, more like it'd been boring. That said, whenever Kail had finished, that had been when I'd vomited every time. Now *that* was gross. What a poisonous jerk, though. He was in college probably living the straight lie, who knew? He'd hurt me, and I'd never forget that.

I sighed. "Yeah."

Geoff focused on me. "Aw, why you are sad?"

"He was a terrible and disgusting person, and very mean to me too. He used me for sex when he led me to believe it'd be more. He only cared about his own needs."

"That boy is not nice. Aw, you need a better boy, Jayden."

"Thanks." I melted in Geoff's arm that still held me, and the more I got to know him and spend time with him, the more I realized just how great he and I were together. I loved Ollie, I really did, and he'd always be the love of my life, but Geoff and I connected in another way that Ollie and I could never do. Geoff was asexual like me, and he was sex-repulsed, which meant I never had to worry about sex, arousals, erections *from* the arousals, and all that boring stuff. It would be only romance and love between us in the future.

But that was thing. He was leaving on New Year's Eve, and I couldn't stop thinking about it. It broke my heart because I was already falling for him. He was such a great guy for me that it was too good to be true. Because of course! Sasha didn't even want me with him in that way, which sucked even more because she couldn't be happy for me.

It wasn't fair!

My eyes watered. "Geoff?"

"Yah?"

After a pause, I turned to face him. "I don't want you to go to Germany. I want you to stay here."

He looked stunned, and I wasn't sure how he'd react. Was I selfish? Was I out of line? I didn't know. I just knew what I felt. It probably wasn't love because it wasn't as strong as what I felt for Ollie, but Ollie wasn't in the picture anymore, and he'd never be in it again. So, Geoff was all I had, and what I felt for him was too special to ignore.

His soft kiss told me he wasn't upset, so that was good. He locked eyes with mine and tried to smile but failed. "You wait for me when I go back to my home?"

That piqued my interest. "What do you mean?"

"When I go back to Germany on December, you're still my boyfriend?"

Oh? Where was *this* headed? And still? What was he implying? "You said 'still' like we're already boyfriends."

"We're not boyfriends?" Geoff looked confused, and that made me confused too.

"I mean…I…did…you *want* to be my boyfriend?"

"I want to, Jayden. I don't make these things with normal friends. I'm on your bed with my underwear here and we make kisses. And you say now that we're not boyfriends?"

"Oh, Geoff, no! I didn't know, I'm sorry!" I kissed him

deeply, and when I let go of his lips, I smiled. "I want to be your boyfriend too. It's just that we never talked about it, but I guess we're officially boyfriends now, right?"

That overjoyed expression on his face told me that I'd just made his day. "You're my first boyfriend, Jayden. And when I go back to Germany, you are still my boyfriend, yah?"

Oh. That. Ugh, the reality. God, what would I do in a long-distance relationship? And were things between us moving a little quickly? "But would I ever see you again after you leave?" I needed to know.

"Yah, but when I'm eighteen years, I come back to Michigan. I talk with my parents, and they have much monies for me to come back here."

Given that Geoff wasn't far from turning sixteen, that would mean a little more than two years, most likely longer if he graduated from his high school in May or June of that year. "So, if we're still boyfriends when you leave for Germany, we won't break up, right?"

"No, Jayden. I don't play those bad games. When I say you're my boyfriend, it's forever. I don't want a temporary boyfriend. No pauses for us."

Oh, Geoff. He continued to be the great guy he really was, and the ideal boyfriend he'd just become a moment ago. Even though I wanted to be his boyfriend, I still had a lot to think about. I liked him too much to lose him, but I also knew that a long-distance relationship could probably be tough. I'd never tried it, but I imagined it'd be. Then again, maybe I could find a way to go to Germany myself.

Maybe I could find a way to get the money somehow. Anything was possible, right?

Or maybe we were moving a bit too fast?

Chapter 25

Halloween was always a fun time of the year, but when living on Lac du Pac Island, watching a horror film was pretty tame, even at night. Sasha, Geoff, and I wanted something scarier that wouldn't be allowed on the island, and in order to watch something like that, it had to be in mainland Michigan. Since the last ferry ride left at five thirty, we had no choice but to watch an earlier show, which was a serious disappointment because watching horror was so much better at night. Otherwise, we'd have to stay at a hotel if we missed the ferry. But why did it have to be a late morning show? That was *too* early.

Sasha also had a surprise for me, but I wasn't sure when I'd get it. She'd said I'd like it and that it hadn't been easy to pull off, so it made me wonder.

The small movie theater was decorated for Halloween, located in a biggish suburb not too far from the ferry docks. While wearing our costumes, we waited in line to buy the tickets to see the new horror film, *Frankenfeaster*. It was expected to be the scariest and goriest of the year. Given the trailer, we'd see about that.

There were lots of people here for the late-morning show, though, which was a surprise. It also meant a crowded theater room because of how small each room was. Hopefully, they would know how to be quiet and actually watch the movie.

"Remember, Jayden," Sasha said with an unpleased expression, dressed as a pastel-haired kawaii girl. "You owe me *bigtime* for making me watch this darker and more twisted Frankenstein remake."

I just had a glittery-pink eye mask with feathers and frills, and an Emma Emmy T-shirt. "Who knows, Sash? It might not be that bad."

"Eh…I don't know about that. He's pretty evil in this movie, like the mad scientist basically invented a killing machine for his twisted pleasure. And he looks *so* creepy and weird, like, ugh." She shuddered. "Plus, it's rated R, so *that* doesn't reassure me because you *know* it'll be gory. If it'd at least been PG-13, it would've been more tolerable."

Geoff formed a confused expression. He was dressed as Zorro. "But I must have seventeen years to watch the movie. ja?"

"Nah, you're fine," Sasha said. "What matters is that one of us is old enough to watch it without having to sneak in."

I grinned. "Like the *one* time?"

Sasha's face flushed, and she shushed me with a giggle after glancing around the lobby.

"Oh, please. They don't have proof." I tried my hardest to have a blast with her, but lying about my new relationship with Geoff made it challenging. I'd tried to limit my time with her because of feeling terrible, and sometimes, I wished I could tell her the truth. If only she could accept it. If only she could realize how happy Geoff made me.

I sighed. "So, when am I going to get my surprise?"

Sasha beamed in a dramatic way. *"Patience is a virtue, little diva,"* she singsonged.

I glanced at Geoff. "Do *you* know what it is?"

He just nodded, and it seemed like something bothered him. What was wrong? Was he not feeling well? I wished we could talk right now, but I'd never abandon Sasha like that.

"Don't tell him, Geoff," Sasha said with a toothy grin.

"I don't say it." Something was definitely bothering him, and it worried me. I was surprised Sasha had been oblivious the whole time.

"Ugh." She rolled her eyes at someone.

I followed her eye direction and noticed Kail's old friends who'd called me mean things in the past. I was surprised that the tough act had shriveled like a balloon the last time Sasha had shown them who was boss.

"Anyway, I'm going to go buy the tickets."

"I'll stay here and wait."

"Yah, me also," Geoff added.

"Okay, I'll be right back." Sasha rushed to the long line and was finally out of earshot.

I gave Geoff my undivided attention and released a big breath. "What's wrong? I know something's up."

He gave me a little frown and looked on the floor. "I can't say it. Sasha's told me not to say nothing."

"You mean, the surprise?"

He nodded.

I was confused because surprises shouldn't have been a bad thing. I wasn't sure what went wrong, but I needed to know. If only he could tell me. After all, we'd been romantically involved in secret, so what difference did it make?

Sasha returned with the tickets.

"How much do I owe you?" I was about to grab my wallet.

Sasha shook her head. "Don't worry about it. My parents gave me money for all of us."

"You sure?"

"Yep, it's on me. Seriously, don't worry about it."

"Thanks."

"You're welcome." Sasha groaned. "Ugh, now I *really* have to go to the bathroom. I'll be back again, sorry." She rushed off.

I nodded and shifted my focus back to Geoff. I didn't want there to be anything wrong with him. Seeing him sad made me feel sad, too, and I wanted to do what I could to cheer him up.

"I go to the toilet also. Be back." He walked away, and it killed me not to know what was up with him. Why couldn't he talk to me? We'd never really had issues before and had always been honest with each other. Why the change?

A guttural sound in disgust ticked my ears. "You're *so* gay."

My gaze landed on a former bully from school who'd already graduated, standing near me with a couple of his buddies whose faces I didn't recognize. My heart pumped faster because I knew there'd be trouble, just as I should've expected whenever Sasha was gone even for a moment. Not even Geoff was here. I was all alone.

Because of course!

"At least hot lesbians have a chance to change with the right guy," he said. "*You* can't no matter how hard you try. I mean, *look* at you and that stupid girly mask. Who got it for you, your sugar daddy?" His face not only matched his tone, but it was difficult to know what he was capable of doing. It was probably the same with his friends.

I swallowed hard and shut my mouth despite my emotions going all over the place. I felt the blood boiling under my skin, and I breathed through my nostrils with tightened lips to prepare myself. "Maybe you should stop hiding and finally come out of the closet, you repressed prick." Ugh, I instantly wished my mouth hadn't slipped. I couldn't help it! It was just like a Kail situation in some ways.

"What did you just say?" The bully pushed me hard.

I fell back but quickly got up, my heart stammering like crazy. I'd never fought in my life, other than slamming my hand against the lockers at Gracie and insulting her, which I still regretted doing. I knew that if I attempted to fight back, there'd be trouble. If only we had security guards the way big cities like Detroit and Grand Rapids did, but *this* little suburb just wasn't built that way.

The bully grabbed me by the shirt collar and gave me the death stare. "Say it again? I want to hear you try to insult me one more time so I can knock you out."

"Hey! Why don't you leave him alone?"

My mouth almost fell open as soon as Ollie showed up out of nowhere with his ticket clutched in his fist. But...*Ollie*? Since *when*? I'd never seen him so bold! It was like some other person had jumped into his body and possessed him. Maybe he'd grown tired of bullies too. He didn't have a costume on because of his religious parents, but he was still as dreamy as ever.

The bully let go of me and focused on Ollie. "Seriously?" He was calm, trying to hold it in.

Ollie's body tensed, and he raised both fists. His eyes locked with the bully's in deep focus. "I practice martial arts, so I'm not afraid of you."

Wait, what...? Why hadn't he ever told me *that*? I managed a slight smile without the others looking, a smile of hope. And to make matters worse, I suddenly missed him like crazy. Was *he* the surprise?

The bully shook his head. "Whatever. You're not worth my time." He walked away, rolling his eyes, and his friends followed him.

My nerves were so wracked that I couldn't even be in the same room with them, but I couldn't exactly abandon Sasha and Geoff. If only the lobby didn't suddenly make me feel emotionally claustrophobic. Who cared about the movie, at this point?

I marched away from my spot and dropped myself on the nearest bench. My face burned with anger and was probably bright red. Being my true self came with a price, but why change to appease the bullies?

"Jayden, hi." Ollie's softened voice soothed my ears. He

sat down next to me. "Relax, okay? Please? Take a deep breath because I can tell you're flustered."

I inhaled and exhaled. "I'm *more* than flustered. I'm *pissed.*"

"I know." He placed a hand on my shoulder and formed a warm smile, and all the memories came flooding back into my thoughts, especially because it hadn't been that long ago since the forced breakup. God, why couldn't I get over him?

"Interesting mask you have," he said.

This touch. This magical touch that didn't just warm me up, but it sent a shock of something nice down my spine and another into my heart. I pursed my lips and breathed through my nostrils until I calmed down. I looked at him and captured his face that suddenly made me smile even harder until I remembered Geoff was still in the building.

"I wish I could wear something," Ollie added. "But, you know, my parents."

"Do they still think Halloween is the Devil's birthday?"

"They do, yes. But it's not a real biggie. I'm used to it since I've never celebrated Halloween in my life. I wouldn't know any different."

It seemed so cruel to deprive a child of something so normal as trick-or-treating, an experience that all kids should have.

"So. Are you better now?"

"Yeah, thanks."

"I was just doing my job, and you're welcome."

"Your job? What, to protect me?" I chuckled.

Ollie sheepishly grinned. "If you want me to, yes. If

not, it's not a real biggie." He let go of my shoulder, and there was a moment of silence.

"Do you really know how to fight like that?" I asked. "Like, karate or whatever?" I still couldn't believe it. It was unreal despite the fact that he'd been athletic. It made sense why his body had changed since freshman year when he'd been lanky and twiggy then.

He nodded. "I do, yes. It's not just karate, actually. There are numerous forms, and many counties have their own, not just the ones in Asia."

"Oh, okay." Like I'd know *that*. "Why didn't you ever tell me any of this? I mean, it's obviously a passion if you're that experienced."

"Jayden, I didn't want you to fear me. I'm very skilled for my level, even though I have a long way to go to earn a black belt."

"But why would I be scared of you?"

"Well, before you and I got close over the summer, I told plenty of people, which was a big mistake. They started fearing me like I was a freak with deadly hands, even though that's far from the case. I'm good, yes, but I'm not *that* good. One of them did call me a freak over it and told me not to come near him."

Aw, poor Ollie. It couldn't have been easy to be rejected like that, but I could relate in a sense, except for different reasons. "I wouldn't have feared you, though."

"Well, I didn't know that at the time. I started feeling like Edward Scissorhands, even though my hands aren't registered to justify it."

I released a giggle while Ollie just sheepishly grinned.

"Did Sasha tell you the surprise?" he asked.

My eyebrows flew up a little. "So, *you're* the surprise?"

"I am, yes. Sasha went to my house to talk to my parents about having me go see a movie with her, except that it was going to be with you and Geoff in secret."

Geoff. God, why? Confusion filled my head, and I didn't know what to do. His disappointment over the surprise suddenly made sense.

Ollie sighed. "Jayden, I miss you so much. Now that I'm allowed to go out with Sasha once in a while since she's a girl, I thought maybe we could make plans to hang out again."

"Oh." I blushed, but my heart raced at the thought of Ollie asking to hangout while not knowing I had a new boyfriend. My heart cracked into many pieces because I didn't want to lose either of them. He'd never forgotten about me, after all. What could I do, though? I couldn't exactly break up with Geoff just like that.

"I want to find a way to spend more time with you. I don't like that I can't talk to you anymore. It just might have to be in the mainland where no one on the island can recognize us. My parents don't trust me going anywhere alone, so seeing me with Sasha makes it believable."

That'd been exactly what I'd dreamed of before I'd gotten involved with Geoff. "Well, I mean, we *are* watching a movie today."

Ollie bit his lower lip and sheepishly grinned. "I got the later show, actually. That was stupid of me, yes. But since the tickets for your movie were sold out, it was the only time

Sasha and I could watch ours together. I didn't think it would be so busy at this time since it's not even noon yet."

I lowered my eyebrows. "Wait, you and Sasha are watching a separate movie together?"

"We are, yes. Right after yours. It's not a horror one or anything unclean, since I'm not allowed to watch those, not that I'm remotely interested."

"That sucks."

"It's not a real biggie. I'm used to it. So. I imagine you and Geoff will have to kill some time while Sasha and I watch our movie."

"I guess." I didn't know what to do anymore. I'd had no idea Ollie would ever show up in my life again. I still loved him, but I was with Geoff now.

"Jayden, I want you back. I want us to be boyfriends again. I couldn't stop thinking about you the entire time we were away from each other."

The feeling of being torn wouldn't leave me alone.

"I never stopped fighting for you, and I never will. You still love me, right?"

What should I do! "Ollie, I…um…"

"Yay, you found the surprise, Jaydles!" Sasha said in a cheerful tone as she approached us with Geoff right behind her. "I'm so animated!"

I glanced at Geoff who looked deeply sad, and I knew I had to talk to him. I couldn't take Ollie back, as much as it pained me to let him go after finally having the chance to be with him again. Ugh, why couldn't it have happened *sooner*?

"He did, yes." Ollie's face was so lit up with excitement

that it only made things worse. He had no idea what had happened while we'd been apart, and Sasha couldn't even know about me and Geoff.

"I bet you're happy, Jayden, aren't you?" Sasha said. She'd always rooted for us to be together, and she still did.

"I hope so," Ollie said while taking my hand and sliding his fingers through mine, and he looked at me as if completely enamored. "I want to be your boyfriend again." He leaned closer to give me a kiss on the cheek, not caring about being seen in this small suburb that wasn't even LGBTQ-friendly.

My heart pounded, and my head hurt from being so torn and confused. When I looked at Geoff, his misty eyes showed so much pain that I was convinced he could cry at any moment. No, I couldn't do this to him. He was my boyfriend, and Ollie and I couldn't be together anymore.

I jolted out of the bench and rushed to Geoff, forcing the most painfully fake smile I could form. "And now it's our surprise, Sasha, but Geoff and I need to talk about it some more."

Sasha looked confused but also intrigued. "Oh…a surprise for me?"

While probably unsuspicious, Ollie did look a bit hurt, most likely from not getting an answer to his loaded question. But I couldn't answer, and it hurt me too.

"Yep! We'll be back!" I gently grabbed Geoff's arm and rushed away from Sasha and Ollie.

"Jayden, I understand if you and Ollie would—"

"No! Stop! Don't even say it. Please? Just…let me find

us some privacy because I *really* need to talk to you. It's important."

Geoff didn't say another word and just followed my lead. I knew he was upset—more than upset. He was probably depressed, and it made sense why something had been bothering him the whole time. He'd known about Ollie being the surprise, and I imagined it cut his heart like a knife.

I turned around a left corner into an empty hallway that led to a side exit, and I stopped near the wall. "Look, Geoff. Ollie wants me back, but I didn't tell him I wanted him or anything like that. He just assumed we'd be back because he knew I loved him."

Geoff's frown deepened. "But you love him still?"

Why did Geoff have to ask me that question? It would only make things worse if I told him the truth. I didn't want to lie, though. "I mean...*yeah*, but it's because it hasn't been that long since we broke up."

"What happens now? Ollie wants again to be your boyfriend, yah?"

I reluctantly nodded. "It was definitely not the surprise I expected. I thought maybe it'd be something tangible, like an object. I'm still shocked."

"I was shocked when she's told me also, but I'm not supposed to discuss something about you and me, so I've had to pretend that there is nothing."

"I get it."

"Ollie is now back. You love him still. And Sasha is so very happy because she wants you and him together. What happens now?"

"I don't know, Geoff. I didn't know he still loved me this whole time." Not that I was surprised.

Geoff's eyes watered. "Ollie is not only the one to love you. I love you also."

Wow, I hadn't expected *that* admission, and it made my heart sink with guilt but also lift with the feeling of being touched. Whether I actually loved Geoff, time would tell, but now, I didn't want to let him go. I pulled him into my arms and kissed him so deeply that I just wanted to forget about the world and be in a heavenly place with him. Our eye masks weren't even in the way, so kissing him was as convenient as it had always been. Thankfully, no one was around at the moment.

I stopped and smiled. "My feelings for you haven't changed, Geoff. You're still my boyfriend, remember? Do you honestly think I'm going to let you go that easily?"

Finally, a little smile curled his lips up, and he kissed me some more. He didn't have to say another word. The moment said it for us, and it spoke loud and clear. Maybe I really did love him too. I didn't know, but there was no rush. New Year's Eve was around the corner, and I wanted to spend what little time I had left with him before I'd have to wait more than two years just to see him again. I loved Ollie, and I might've loved Geoff too. Unfortunately, despite having had a touchy-feely sweet thing with both guys, I could only choose one of them.

But I still wanted both.

About Kieran Frank

I am a gay fiction author of sweet romance, young adult, asexual, and inspirational. My heroes always have their beautiful happily-ever-after, but a happy-for-now works in some cases.

More From Deep Hearts YA

The Mixtape to My Life
Jake Martinez

Justin has always been comfortable in his skin, even if the world around him wasn't. A junior simply counting down the days for when he can leave for college, Justin's life is thrown for a loop when the one thing that helps him feel like himself suddenly slips away from him. But an unexpected blast from his past puts summer on a new and exciting path, one as random and unexpected as a mixtape.

Gay Love and Other Fairy Tales
Dylan James

What starts with a surprise kiss leads to a year of shared secrets, hidden love, relationship troubles, and broken hearts. For football captain Benjamin Cooper and his secret boyfriend, cheer co-captain Jordan Ortiz, there's only one thing standing in the way of their love—Ben's intense need to stay closeted, a need that just might tear them apart.

L.I.F.E.
Felyx Lawson

Rider is a closeted high school student and would be happy to stay that way, if not for two obstacles in his path: an assignment about love, and Cameron Walker, a new student who is so much more than the jock he first appears to be.